Children of Silthar

Everett L. R. Asher

Copyright © 2023

All Rights Reserved

Table of Contents

Dedicated to Jason Zedaker, my uncle, not by blood.

Without whom, my obsession with the fantasy genre would

be but distant echoes.

I only wish you could have read it. I think you would have

loved it...

Acknowledgements

On this maiden voyage, I would like to take some time before the story begins to give proper thank-yous to those that have given something to help make this book happen. First and foremost, I would like to thank Blake Rathie, who edited this mess and found a diamond in this heap. A writer is only as good as their editor; this is a phrase I will take with me to my grave.

I would also like to thank Amanda Jewell, the first of the beta readers, for taking time out of her day and tell me her thoughts and opinions on my book. It's one thing for someone I'm paying to tell me that it's good, but it's another when someone I ask on a whim enjoys it. You also gave me the greatest compliment a writer could ever receive: "I was getting ready to fall asleep, but I just couldn't put the book down."

I would also like to thank the wonderful folks at NaNoWriMo, without whom this novel wouldn't exist in the first place. I set out to write a book in a month, and while it's not industry standard length for a fantasy novel, I still think it deserves its time in the sun.

To Mrs Drennan of my 3rd grade school year, I give my thanks for seeing potential in me that I didn't even acknowledge until my freshman year of high school. While sifting through old relics of the past, I found one of my old school notebooks. She gave a note that reads: 'You are becoming a great writer!' After years of self-doubt, seeing such a note in one of my old notebooks that she saw potential in paragraphs riddled with grammatical errors was refreshing. I don't know how she saw that in a child at such a young age, but I cannot thank her enough.

About the Author

Throughout his childhood, Everett always knew he had a spark of creativity. Yet, for the longest time, he never knew how he would choose to express that creativity. It wasn't until he read *Dracula* by Bram Stoker that he knew he wanted to be a writer and author. Since then, he has made it a personal goal to become an author. It's his passion and his dream job.

Chapter One: Not Living, Not Dead

Esta Desidarius

As the sun died, the servants of blood feasted upon their dead god. Esta could hear their distant jubilant cries as they savoured the taste of their deity's essence. Centuries had passed since it had fallen at their first ruler's hands. Slew out of dissatisfaction and power lust despite their granted freedom.

Esta boasted a meal not nearly as glamorous; she could still taste the sour blood of the dead rat in her mouth.

She sat amongst familiar shadows, the sun descending just beyond the distant mountains. The bleeding rays danced against her skin as they bled through the small crevice to the outside world, causing a numb sting to wash over her. Esta did not mind the pain they brought; it was the only thing that kept her from going insane or worse.

It painted the sands in blood red, noble amethyst, and bright yellow. The red sands reminded her of home, of Rath. In her mind, she could remember the cool nights with her brothers hunting for their dinner. She remembered the days when she would serve in battles against the enemies of her people, their blood soaking in the sands that would forget them. She almost forgot her time with Ezran, her twin brother. Those were cold days in a festering hell.

The half-elf clenched her right hand and the now-weakened sword arm. The distant memory of holding a weapon gnawed at her psyche. There persisted a bitter emptiness, a void that demanded to be filled. She still remembered the reconditioning she endured before her enslavement. The scarab buried in her head buzzed, reminding her of her subservience, drawing back buried memories she wished were only nightmares.

For months she endured the agony of nearly losing every ounce of her sanity to the torture of the Skithik. A new slave of the Skithik is first supposed to endure relentless feedings from the other slaves. Next, they are turned and subsequently killed, left to endure the madness of vampirism as it invades their minds and changes their demeanour, turning them into monsters. The hunger overtakes all needs or wants, then finally, they have the scarab burrow into their neck and succour most of their sustenance of blood. They are left to exist in the grey area of life and death, devoid of purpose and drive but still capable of what the Skithik demand.

Beyond the walls of her crevice, she heard all manner of sickening actions. Sad and weary souls, broken and crying out for mercy. Should she ever consider this to be her home, the madness would have then surely overtaken her. Endure; the only hope that existed in the bleak, damp walls of the Arteries, such a den of depravity and primal hunger. Her resolve to survive waned.

Esta tossed her drained breakfast into the shadows. She could see clearer now; the blinding rays of the sun now fell beneath the horizon. The nook she called 'home' was perhaps big enough for four other inhabitants, yet none ever entered to prove such a theory. She counted herself lucky to have such solace away from the dark deeds that unravelled daily in the Arteries. She always heard the screams of pain and suffering in the winding and the nigh endless network of caves. The maddening endless nature of the Arteries gave meaning to its name. She always felt trapped in the heart of a blackened beast.

Esta shuffled over to a small pool of water collected from a small leak in her nook. Before she plunged her hands into the cold pool, she saw her reflection. Her knotted ebony locks cascaded off her shoulders and nearly touched the surface of the water. Her bright scarlet eyes stared back at her, above sunken cheeks, burning with hatred and hunger. She had not seen how emaciated she was until she saw her reflection. She bit her cracked lip as she gazed at someone she could not help but convulse.

As always, the scarab hummed to life, draining the essence that settled in her stomach. She hated it, all of it. She hated the scarab that took the majority of her new form of sustenance. She hated the sickness that roiled in her veins, the noxious venom that held her in this awful transient state. She hated that she could not feel the warm kiss of the sun upon her skin, only to be reminded of the grave's cold and refusing call. She hated that she forgot what food tasted like. She hated that her training as a soldier had slipped into a nearly forgotten corner of her mind. Esta did as much as she could to retain a small inkling of skill, the weight of slavery reflected on her thinner muscles. Each day she felt another piece of herself slip away into oblivion until only a shell of herself remained. Despair found its home within her, the embers of hope clung to life, but it faded with each passing day.

A buzz brought her thoughts out of the stupor of self-hatred, the numbing pain livening her. Her reptilian masters had returned. It was time for her to work.

Cupping her hands, she tossed the water against her face and washed them clean of the blood that had already begun to dry.

Gathering herself, Esta shuffled to the edge of her nook, peeking over the edge. Countless tunnels dotted every corner of the Arteries' circular chamber. Bridges crisscrossed over its sandstone walls, connecting tunnel to tunnel. Arterians, the vampire slaves, scuttled about, crawling on walls or shuffling on wounded feet. Of all races and kinds, they wore torn rags on their broken bodies and madness in their scarlet eyes.

The scarab's buzzing grew in intensity. It was the second wave sent out to have all of the Arterians focus on their approaching masters.

On the chamber's far wall, she watched the Skithik enter. Lithe muscular beasts, two metres tall, with webbed hands and feet, fins protruding from their heads and backs, and tails. The Skithik's mortal hearts still pumped with fresh blood. Not partaking in the feasting of their god's power struck Esta as odd.

Their scales appeared smooth and slick with some form of mucus substance, similar to a frog. Yet the cruelty in their eyes as they hissed and snapped their toothy maws at the Arterians perished any similarity to such gentle creatures.

They wrapped themselves in scale mail, rusted and dusty from the desert they lived in. Their weapons were ready and flailed as they ordered the Arterians to fall in line.

She obeyed like the rest, crawling along the chamber wall towards the main bridge. Her eyes on the Skithik all the while.

Three hundred Arterians gathered upon this bridge, cramped and pressed to the edge, Esta knew more Arterians persisted within these tunnels, but the Skithik slavers seemed satisfied with their number. The buzz in the back of Esta's neck ceased, and her mind regained the freedom to escape back to the days she spent in the rank and file of the Eternium's army, the coalition of nations between the Elves, Dwarves, and Humans. It was not often a half-elf found themselves in their midst, but it was the only place she knew she could call her home. It was the only place left that accepted her.

Esta closed her eyes for a moment, allowing her distant memories to fade back into her subconscious. She moved her gaze over the throng of her fellow Arterians, connecting her gaze upon the most zealous of all the slaves.

She was tall, with elegant features. A sharpened and noble countenance that dubbed her amongst the beauty of the elves, though her ears that protruded from her silver locks did more than enough to notify all of her status and her ancestral origins. Similar to the many Arterians around, her irises stained a dark red, stark against her porcelain skin.

Esta curled her lip in anger. Sana Nailo was her name. She was one of the Sanguinaire, a vampiric sub-race of elves. Long ago, the Sanguinaire was chosen by Silthar, God of Blood and Lineage, to be his chosen followers. There was a difference between Arterians and the Sanguinaire, the likes of which Esta could not ascertain.

Sana bled with zealotry and often preached to the fellow Arterians. Esta clenched her jaw and rested her hand over the ancestral mark of her half-elven clan. Her ancestral mark took the form of a hawk head, with the rising sun behind it. She sighed, squeezing her marked shoulder.

Sana never met eyes with Esta. Her focus was on the small retinue that followed her every whim. Like a shepherd, they flocked to her, accepting her generous offers of blood that she collected and dispensed to her followers. They would fight for her, for an Arterian that is no more powerful than any other. Yet still, they flock to her like she is some manner of messiah that would keep them safe and would free them from their enslavement.

The Skithik darted their attention over the throng of Arterians. From the language difference and their cold reptilian demeanors, Esta could not tell why they looked amongst themselves, and the Arterians gathered. Counting, perhaps? Intimidating?

After enduring their cold reptilian stares for a few minutes, they hissed and clicked their hideous language.

Esta crossed her arms, her studious gaze moving to one of the Arterians that addressed her, "What are they doing?"

He was a human, twenty at Esta's best guess, with a strong, stocky frame. He might have been a farmer of some kind before his fate of becoming an Arterian. She peered deep into his eyes. They welled with innocence. She always envied that. The ignorance of not knowing what horrible atrocities awaited all in the outside world. Anger, war, retaliation, conquest, genocide, despair, and madness; the list went on. Others like him gave her the answer she needed as to why she endured so much hardship; to maintain their innocence as best she could. He must have been new.

She did not move her head to connect eyes, focusing on the Skithik as she said, "Wish I knew."

Her voice, she noticed, became more hoarse as time went on. Scratchy at times but still harboured what small amount of stern tenor she knew to be her own.

The human rubbed his hands together. Nervousness bled from him as he shook out, "By the Pantheon, what will they do with us?"

His question was answered as they all sheathed their weapons, procured whips, and began shouting at them. Thunderous cracks erupted in the still and quiet air of the Arteries. Double the length of their impressive heights, they struck multiple Arterians. Well practised, they made sure every Arterian received the cracking of their whips. The sting from the whips that struck against her skin, as it always had been, stung deeper than her flesh. She could feel the cruel hatred of the Skithik in their strikes.

They pointed to the far exit, where they had come from, whipping and shoving the throng of slaves towards it. Trudging towards another night of back-breaking work. As she slinked her way towards the door, she could not shake the feeling that Nosgora would be much kinder than what she endured now. She welcomed it.

The human male stumbled, pushed by one of the other Arterians, but foolishly nudged against one of the Skithik slavers.

Whipping around, the Skithik threw the human Arterian to the floor, raising his whip to punish the Arterian.

Esta stepped in front of the human and stood defiant against the snarling lizard guard. His whip still came down. The whip wrapped around her, constricting her in a stinging embrace. Burns erupted around her as the blessed silver whip struck her. She could feel her wounds begin to fester and boil.

Again the whip came down and collided against her skin, rising in pain once more, and because of the proximity to the other wounds, they both rose in heat and boiled on her flesh.

With each lashing, she felt her consciousness slip. She struggled against the pain of enduring lashings that the farm boy did not deserve. There was no active resistance on her part to remain conscious. With all of her heart, she secretly begged for the darkness to overtake her vision.

She fell to her knees, her form wobbling and her eyes cloudy with the creeping spectre of unconsciousness racking her brain.

A force connected against her cheek, scaly and hardened with sadistic cruelty.

Her head followed the force, nearly taking her to the ground. Repressed memories of all the times she had nearly been knocked out, all those times when she struggled against falling to unconsciousness. Repressed memories of war, death, and blood rose within her mind. Memories of showering in the rising tide of blood as she fell one foe after another. Blood that she cherished.

Through the haze, she felt the Skithik slaver grab the cuff of her ragged shirt. The old stained cloth nearly tore at the seams from the force. She groaned in pain. His hot breath wreathed her face. Her puffy eye had already started to heal, and she saw razor-sharp rows of teeth centimetres from her face.

She heard the hunger in his voice as he threatened in broken common, "Next time… the Pit."

Esta spat on the ground, the taste of iron lingering on her tongue. The edges of her vision returned to normal as she stood up, rolling her shoulders. The pain in her back slowly fading with each second.

The Pit was where the Skithik housed all of the problematic slaves. Even from a distance, she could hear the tortured screams of those who found themselves there. During the day, they are left out in the baking sun, forced to mine silver. She had heard of countless other depraved acts that the Arterians forced upon each other. Thinking of herself among them made her shiver with fear.

The Skithik slaver whipped her and handed her off to two others who breathed with the same hunger.

The first said, "She… pull stone."

With those words, she knew where they were going to corral them in the mines of Ardarian. More repressed memories flooded her mind, and those torturous months came back to her.

The hunger amongst them became obvious as the one to her left said, "Not done."

He shoved her through the gathering Arterians and handed her off to the human for whom she took the lashings and threatened, "Hold... her."

He seized her arms and forced her to her knees.

She closed her eyes just as the tide of pain showered over her back once more. Each strike felt like a new facet of hatred opened from the cruel and cold hearts of the reptilian slavers. Each strike brought her closer to unconsciousness, and she could not help but want, in her heart of hearts, to slip away.

Tears welled in her eyes. She craved death, anything that could take her far away from this hell. Her back felt slick and wet with blood. Ezran could fight this. He was strong enough to steel his resolve and defy the Skithik.

Choking through tears, she whispered, "I can't..."

Esta did not feel it when they stopped. Her back felt as if it had been burned with white-hot flames. She violently shook as her body struggled against the silver-tipped whips that struck against her.

As her body started to heal, Esta's eyes clenched shut against the tide of pain. She remained there as the Skithik ordered the Arterians to fall out. She dreaded what awaited her. Tears fell freely from her. Nothing could have prepared her for cruelty on this level, not even the punishment she faced upon exile from Rath.

Life itself was pain for an Arterian, a life that Esta loathed.

Chapter Two: Where Shadows Linger

Sana Nailo

As night settled, Sana's muscles ached at the memories of oppressive labour. She trudged with the rest of the Arterians. She hated that word. She was no Arterian. She was a Sanguinaire, the heirs to the fallen elven empire and she was subservient to no one. Her defiance is what brought her through the agony and the torture they all had to endure. Though she viewed herself as separated from her Arterian kin, she knew that the pain they all went through had bound them. A crucible of torture that no one alive or dead could compare to, a fate worse than death. She could use this to set them free.

She remembered when she was taken captive. Sana had decided to visit her father, Silas Nailo, on the mainland. Sana prepared for a short trip while on their way from Dawnshade Harbor on the south side of Nostra. A storm caught them and a ship belonging to the Skithik took advantage of it while the crew was scrambling to board and take all they could. They took everything except for the floorboards, leaving the Nostrian vessel for the sea to swallow. She could never shake the failure of being captured so easily, just as she could not shake the unease at the strangeness of the letter her father sent. It claimed that he needed aid in establishing a trade agreement with King Valamer Ostrogoth, yet he was the Nightlord. He knew much more about trading than anyone. Being the oldest in the lands of Calisine with more than ten thousand years of existence, it was hard to believe that he could not establish a simple trade deal. He saw kingdoms rise and fall, the start and end of countless wars for misbegotten reasons. He sought counsel with Gods and faced otherworldly evils without fear, and yet he asked her aid to establish a simple trade route.

The secrets she knew, the power he wielded with his sword alone; the infamous Kal'Drae. She never felt the shame that he did; of their stained heritage. Her mother often reminded him of the purpose of that action. Without it, the plane of Calisine would not be the same, yet he always wore that shameful look.

Sana gathered herself out of her memory and inhibitions, drinking in the scenery of the night. Stars burst with ancient light, dazzling and dancing across the nebulous sky. The vastness of the sky was painted with strokes of bright blue, warm amber and a blended violet. At another time, Sana would have drunk in sight. Even her centuries-old self still admired the beauty of the night sky. To some, it bothered them that they could not see the daylight sky. It did not bother Sana. She loved the way the night, the Great Tapestry, would talk and tell stories through the constellations.

Their Skithik masters hissed and slurred, gathering Sana's attention. She turned and saw two Arterians. The pitiful one was upon the sands, blood rushing from a bright red wound across the length of his cheek. Tears welled in his innocent eyes. The other was her, Esta Desidarius.

She stood defiant against their reptilian masters, a raised arm taking the brunt of the whippings. Standing up for the weak, but why? Sana heard that the half-elf had the same hair colour as her twin brother, jet black. From one look at her, one could surmise her knowledge of war was not limited. Her frame was stern, her muscles toned but not bulging, whatever remained of them at least. This told all of her extensive training in the countryside of the Red Desert, Rath. Her bright red rebellious eyes were bursting with hatred and vengeance.

That name, Desidarius, harboured the weight of great destiny, any who carry that name were born and bred to carry out great deeds. Esta was no different, she was the twin of Ezran Desidarius, a paragon of justice and law. They both served in the Olkhan Invasion when Kodlan Khane, the God-Killer, threatened to overtake the lands of the humans with his horde of orcish raiders. Ezran was a former Warden, an order so secret that Sana only knew of their existence because her father mentioned them and from the legends surrounding Ezran. He challenged Kodlan Khane to a duel. Neither won but what mattered was that Ezran landed a wound. Up until that point, it was believed that no mortal could wound the God-Killer. This demoralised his followers, causing the invasion to end fairly soon after.

Another Skithik joined and forced Esta to her knees, lashing her back. She groaned and yelped at the pain.

Sana shook her head. Her futile attempt to stand up for one that could barely take care of themselves as noble but ultimately ended with only Esta receiving the punishment. Sana saw no reason for it other than to prove others that she was willing to take the punishment for anyone that she saw and believed was being treated unjustly. It was a way for others to take advantage of her. That was what Sana saw. Either that, or she wanted to die by someone else's hands.

She was on her hands and knees, clutching at the blood-soaked sands, tears welling in her eyes. The wounds would heal, eventually. With vampirism, there was no permanent scarring or lingering wounds, but the memory of the pain never left, which was the greatest punishment of all.

They lifted her to her feet, who barely remained conscious, dragging her with them as they bid everyone else to continue on to their destination.

One of the Arterians that called themself her follower piped up and said, "Would you do that for us, milady?"

Sana turned towards the owner of the voice. It was a halfling girl. With only a glance, she could see the influence of the fae on the ancestry of the halflings. She was more petite for a halfling, with muted red hair and pale, freckled features. Onora Fleetfoot was her name.

She said, the royal tone of her voice keeping quiet amongst the din of the Arterians, "She wants freedom, as we all do. And she believes that death can grant her that. A Soldier that craves death, not of others but themselves, are a dangerous lot. Their suicidal nature could be misread as bravery or honor, but in the end, that's what they want – their end. Punishments are our own to carry, not someone else's. I would avenge you instead."

Onora said nothing and nodded.

Sana returned her gaze to the face ahead of them. She had no intentions of being kept a slave to the wills of the Skithik. She would find a way to escape and return to her people to find her father. Somehow…

They were brought to a sandstone mine that the Skithik used to build all of their structures. It was located only a mile or so out of the port city they called Ardarian. This was the hub where slaves were being bought, sold, and traded. They bought slaves and would then be taken to one of the main cities further inward and for further reconditioning. Sana counted herself lucky not to have been one of those sorry lots.

To call Ardarian a port city would be generous. There were structures that kept it aloft that stood against the harsh desert winds, but they were ramshackle, to say the least. The elements would weather them down to such a degree that the Arterians would often have to rebuild the town. Whether this was purposeful, Sana did not know, but it was too coincidental not to see it that way.

Their job at the sandstone mine was simple enough; carve stones about four metres in length and bring them to Ardarian. There they would either be put on a ship to be sold elsewhere or taken back to the capital. Despite their strength, they would often take hours to cut the stones and load them onto the ships.

Sana's pickaxe was brought up and came down with great force. The other Arterians did the same. Their strikes were not in unison but followed in a similar rhythm. Their stone neared completion.

Sana paused, brushing her fingers against the scarab on her neck. Clenching the pickaxe tighter in her hand, she considered this moment to escape.

The scarab tightened its grip on her neck, perishing the thought. There must have been some sort of spell that prevented her from consciously removing the scarab.

Sana continued to strike, moving her gaze over to the slaves that would lift the stone blocks. She watched as they hooked up a rig around Esta and a few other poor chosen souls. Their job was the hardest. They were hooked up to a large pulley where they would lift the heavy stone to the top of the large mine. It had already reached nearly a mile in height. Sana's back ached at the thought.

The only break they had was when the Arterians hoisted the stones. As she heard the groaning and screaming of pain in the mines, Sana looked around herself.

The Skithik doubled their numbers now. The mines were a popular site for Arterians to run. Many escaped their clutches at the mines, their fate unknown to the other Arterians. It also remained the only site that offered the most space for them to keep the Arterians in line.

She watched their interactions. They were speaking candidly and whispering amongst each other. This was odd to Sana. They were an often boisterous group that did not care if the Arterians could hear them. They could not understand them anyway, so what was the point in lowering their voice?

Her acute elven hearing picked up a word that existed outside of their language, not any word but a name, Ostrogoth. The former ancestral line that controlled Aebolon, the heartland of the human empire. It was not Valamar. He was assassinated a few years prior, along with most of his heirs. Why did they mention his family name? Sana knew about the Night of the Black Swords from one of her father's occasional letters. Gruesome was the only word she had to describe the event.

She snapped back as she heard a pulley break. She watched as the stone plummeted numerous feet above their heads and pulverised the one underneath it. The grim sound echoed in the mines, making Sana wince.

The Skithik shouted, with their harsh language, and ordered a few Arterians to grab it and push it up the other way, up the carved ramps. The other three attached to the pulleys finished hoisting their stones. Sana found herself admiring strengths of Esta as she hoisted her stone. Despite the lashings, she carried on with her task. It was a true testament to the name Desidarius.

The throng of Arterians moved again, going up the ramps to the awaiting stones. Sana searched through the throng and found Esta, who was still recovering from her lashings a few hours earlier. She did not know if it was a gruesome interest that Sana sought her out in the crowds of the Arterians or something else. She did not care for Esta, but her deeds proved to Sana and all that she rightly bore the weight of her ancestral name. If they were to have any chance of escaping the cruel Skithik, Sana suspected Esta would be pivotal in their release.

In the small hours, while she worked, she analysed her dreams, broken and distorted as they were, in an attempt to garner any amount of truth from them.

She saw a plane of bare obsidian rock with rivers of roiling blood. A lone man stood, tall and proud, amongst others that shuffled towards him and prayed. They bowed to him, who was shrouded in a cloak of darkness and wore worn steel armour upon his arms and legs. His chest was bare, revealing cracked and desiccated skin. A wound that festered and glowed with scarlet energy on his sternum. Seeing the wound, she knew this man to be the Shepherd of Blood, Silthar.

Dreaming of the Gods was typically a sign of favour, a sign that they needed help. The Pantheon was forbidden from physically manifesting on the material plane, yet they could circumvent this rule by using mortals as their avatars and conduits for their power. What struck Sana as odd was the fact that Silthar already had two avatars to use at his disposal, Enoch the Nocturnal and her father, Silas Nailo. Granted, her father *had* gone missing a few months ago, but that did not mean that he lost favour with Silthar. It all seemed very odd.

Chapter Three: In the House of Blood

Esta Desidarius

Though the wounds had healed, her soul rent with the strikes of hatred and the promise of evermore agony. Esta lumbered with the other Arterians as they made their way back into the Arteries. The weight of her wounds threatened to pull her into the grave and tear her soul apart. Death lingered, mocking her. Reminding her of the fate that she could never have. They would not waste a life such as hers, there was still work to be done and they were never satisfied.

As they entered the main chamber of the Arteries, she felt her vampirism gnaw at the edges of her psyche. The curse never fully set in, leaving them all in a primal state of endless hunger. It was everything that drove them. Whenever it arose that they were being fed, only primal instincts lurched them forward. The new Aterians that were going through the first stage of their reconditioning were simultaneously her most hated feeding and her most treasured. The taste of mortal blood, not the rats that she needed because there was nothing else but the mortal essence she cherished and would savour the taste every time.

In her drunken stupor, she did not hear her initially, but she could tell that someone was trying to get her attention and she said, "What?"

Sana said nothing, she seemed to have trailed off, but Esta could see the judgement in her eyes. She likely saw what she had done and had some 'wisdom' she wanted to pass on.

Esta clenched her hand as Sana replied, "You aren't alone in your pain. You know that."

"Keep your sermon to your followers. They'll fall on deaf ears if you give them to me."

The half-elf looked briefly at Sana, who folded her hands and thought for a moment and replied, "This blessing—"

Esta pushed forward, her faux blood boiling, "Why do you care? You believe me to be important? You think that just because I took lashings for someone that didn't deserve it that I am some sort of lost child for you to shepherd? Keep your indoctrination to yourself."

One belonging to her retinue stepped forward and said, "Mind your tongue! You have no—"

"I don't recall asking for your input, drone!" Esta barked, thoroughly silencing him.

Sana stepped closer, bearing down on the half-elf, but Esta just tightened her gaze as the elf said in a cool and even tone, "Don't take my words to be against you. I am not your enemy. Our enemies are the ones that gave you unneeded wounds. You're attracting a lot of attention to yourself. I am just trying to tell you that there is hope if we work together. Because we—"

Esta slammed her balled fist against the side of Sana's face, connecting with her cheek with great force. Against a normal mortal, it would have most assuredly knocked them out or worse. Esta had wanted to do that for months now. It felt quite relieving.

She recoiled from the blow, raising her hand as her followers were ready to pounce upon Esta. However, Esta was not afraid. In the back of her mind, she hoped that Sana's followers would just tear her to shreds. Her sanity peeled back for a moment as she shouted, "There is no we! There is no hope! Stop trying to install false hope in everyone's minds of a rebellion that will never take place. You are not the misbegotten princess of the Sanguinaire. You are not important. You are just a husk, like the rest of us!"

Sana pursed her lips for a moment, with no words and fast as lightning, she struck Esta across the cheek as well. Nails dug into her cold flesh, the sting lighting up her cheek in pain. It was nothing compared to what she endured earlier in the night.

She stumbled back, dancing near the edge of the bridge they stood upon. With the back of her hand, she wiped some of the blood off of her cheek. An ancient need rose within her, a primordial hunger for violence. A feeling she had not felt in years, not since the Olkhan Invasion.

No words were exchanged. They both understood what was about to happen now as they both went into threatening stances.

Esta was the first to strike, lunging forward with her sharpened nails out, poised to rend flesh. Sana being more seasoned and familiar with their shared curse, dodged and avoided each of her swipes. Her anger raged like a boundless flame, urging her muscles on. She could feel the vampirism, locked away so deep within her that it caused the scarab to buzz. It craved violence, for blood to spill and satiate her. Sana found an opening with her strikes and landed a jab into her ribcage. The force that collided with her side caused a pause in her assault. She landed another jab against Esta's chin, her head wheeling from the force. Her vision blurring, the anger within her raged with more intensity, but she knew deep within that this battle was fruitless. She was centuries older than Esta. All those centuries, she knew and was familiar with the vampiric curse. There was nothing that Esta could do to break her seasoned defence. So she decided to do something so unpredictable that it shocked her. Esta charged with unbridled fury in her eyes and tackled Sana, grabbing her tight and forcing them both off the bridge. As they plummeted off the side, she heard the distant gasps of Sana's followers and the other onlookers.

Sana tried to rip herself free, her eyes wide with fear as she shouted, "What are you doing!?"

Esta felt deep pain and gave her answer, her eyes welling as she said, "Freeing us both from this gods-forsaken place…"

She did not let go of the elven vampire. Looking down at the bottom of the chamber, she saw a sea of bones. Death lingered with them, plummeting to the bottom, waiting for them to meet the grim aspect of unlife.

All thoughts, all muscles seized as the base of her neck bashed against one of the lower bridges. In a quick flash, all life ceased. Esta relished the freedom of pain.

***

Sana's fear surmounted, and an unearthly crunching of bones and flesh erupted in her acute ears. The muscles against her let her go as life slipped from the veins of Esta Desidarius.

Free from the tightening hold of Esta, she looked up to her followers once more, what assuredly would be the last time she would see them. She said to herself, "Silthar… guide them and forgive me for failing to find the purpose of my vision… forgive—"

She was cut off as her head as well collided with a rock, ending everything in a single painful moment.

***

No pain bid her rise, but Esta felt herself awaken. What happened? She assured herself that she had died.

Confused, she lifted herself up onto soft and cold obsidian stone, her mind wracking around what had happened. Shaking her consciousness back to her.

Blinking furiously, she looked about herself and felt her breath catch as she saw a black sky fill her vision above, with clouds that appeared to be open gashes of bright red. She felt the distant life that it had. It murmured softly and many of them did. Formless vampiric blood maddeningly talked with one another in a language she could not help but recognise.

Holding onto the fringes of her sanity, she looked to the vast grounds that sprawled out for nigh endless kilometres, and around her was a river of bright crimson that split into various tributaries beyond her foreseeable sight. It moved slowly but not like water. No, her mind succumbed to her base desires as she realised what these rivers were.

She charged forward with reckless abandon, kneeling at the banks of the rivers of scarlet. She licked her lips as the vampirism within her bid her to drink from its bottomless depths. Handfuls after handfuls, she scooped the blood from the river, coating her fingers and her palms. She felt herself filling with power and satiation. This blood was unlike any she had tasted before. She felt herself moaning at the heavenly taste.

Esta slapped her hand on the back of her neck, a growl hanging in her throat. But the weight was absent. In her plummet to the ground below, the scarab must have been destroyed.

Her veins livened as she continued engorging herself on the river of blood, a feeling she had not felt since her enslavement to the Skithik. The primal throes of her curse ceased and her mind cleared for once in maddening months. The weight in her neck was absent and the freedom filled her veins just as the rivers of life essence flowed through.

Licking her hands clean of the crimson ambrosia, she looked and saw her drinking from the rivers as well. *Sana Nailo.*

Gently bringing her cupped hands to her lips as she sipped the blood. Finishing her meal, Esta dragged her tongue across her lips, "Why do you drink so politely?"

Sana answered, there was no tension between them as she shrugged, "Easier to clean."

Esta shrugged as well and stood up. She refused to allow Sana to dampen her elation. Stretching her strengthened veins, she said, "Where are we?"

"Ebrithaera," Sana said, her lips savouring the name as she continued, "The afterlife that awaits all vampires. Owned by Silthar, the God of Lineage and blood. The Father of the Bloodlines."

Esta nodded to herself. A deep sadness crept in, knowing that she was robbed of the afterlife promised to all half-elves, not by any of the Gods, but of her ancestry. Her ancestral mark upon her left shoulder now burned with shame, another rising point of self-hatred.

Wiping her stained hands against the stone, Esta said, "Don't know what I was expecting, but it wasn't this."

Sana cleaned her hands as well and replied, "Perhaps you should have listened to my sermons. I was doing that to prepare them for the afterlife that faced them."

Esta set her jaw and whispered to herself, "Guess I just didn't want to believe it."

They were both urged to turn by something, an awakening presence of untold control.

As she did, she saw a distant, nightmarish castle, not unlike one seen in the dark forests of Revendor. A towering obsidian monolith with an expansive opening with no gate. Distantly she saw figures walking towards the huge opening.

Then she saw him, the unfathomably large figure, vaguely human in appearance. A black cloak shrouded its lower half unbidden by the warm winds that rushed by. Its skin was an ashen grey, sunken, and with barely any life clinging to its huge bones, carved into its sternum was a wound that appeared to be in the form of a dagger pointing to his chest. A deep scarlet glow emanated from the wound. Esta now noticed that all the rivers of blood were coming from that wound on his chest. Draped over its sunken and near lifeless face was a veil of muted blond hair, skin formed over its lips. Protruding from its back were black length-less wings that devoured the sky behind him.

In its hand was a sword that was driven into the ground. Two horns burst from its head, curling back at the top with etchings along its length. The runic language was ancient. Esta dared not to read it any more than she had to.

It sat atop the gate that Esta now noticed was its obsidian throne. The sight killed any words she had, never had she witnessed such a horrifying sight. Sana had joined her side and pushed her to her knees as the form turned its gaze towards them, "Kneel before him."

She did and heard a deep and rumbling voice in her head. *"Ah, my Chosen. You have finally found your way to my gates. I bid you welcome to my house of blood."*

Silthar paused, then Sana whispered to Esta, "Let me do all of the talking."

Esta nodded and watched the exchange, still awestruck by Silthar.

Sana said, nearly shouting, "Silthar, grand-father of blood and vampires, we are but your humble servants."

Silthar answered, "We have little time, my chosen, so I will be brief. The reptilian abominations that dare use vampirism in such an accursed way must be wiped from the face of Calisine. I would employ my Hands, but they have left my favour. Enoch the Nocturnal turns to demonic forces and wishes nothing but unrelenting war and blood, conspiring with the reptilian filth. And Silas Nailo is nowhere to be found, for not even I can see where he has gone."

He paused for a moment, and Sana audibly gulped.

Silthar continued, "So I must name my new hands, to which I have chosen you two. Sana Nailo and Esta Desidarius. You both will carry my name with you as you cleanse the lands of the Skithik filth."

He paused again, waiting for them to give some sort of answer. Esta did not know whether to feel pride or shame as she not only had taken the curse of vampirism but also became the chosen hand of the God of Blood himself. It all felt too much.

Sana did not have the same feelings as she said, "We are humbled and honoured that you have chosen us as your hands. We shall prove ourselves worthy of the titles you have bestowed upon us."

Esta remained silent, not wishing to insult the God.

"The more you resist the blessing of vampirism, the more it will consume you, Esta. Do not fail me, my chosen. Go forth back to the blighted lands of Urstron and destroy the memory of the Skithik. Prince Vedus Ostrogoth is the key to

your success. Without him, your crusade against the Skithik will be a farce. Only by his hand can the last of the Skithik be vanquished."

Esta heard him whisper in her mind, *"Do not prove me wrong in choosing you, heroborn!"*

With those last words, she felt her body crumble to the ground. Unconsciousness gripping her once more, the blackness shrouded her eyes and her mind as she fell from the plane of blood.

Chapter Four: Baptised In Shadows

Vedus Ostrogoth

He screamed from the cradle of death. The volume of his yell shook the stone walls around him. His catharsis of shadows peeled away from his sight. Drenched in the damp cold of sweat and dew from stone, Vedus shuttered from the bidding to be filled with life again and the biting winds of the cavern.

The young prince strained with all his might against chains, his wrists bound to an upright stone table. He shook the bindings best he could, but nothing could release him from their titanic grip.

His screaming subsided and heavy gasps replaced the cries of rebirth. His mind drowned in questions. His body felt barely functional, the chill of death lingering on his bones.

He looked about in the darkness, trying to find something or anything that he could talk to so he could get the answers he sought. He heard nothing but loud whispers and exchanges, but as he looked around, he saw no one. They did not cease, no pause for reflection, only the deafening voices that threatened to tear apart his sanity.

"SILENCE!" He shouted at the top of his lungs, his voice torn and hoarse from the constant use at extreme volumes. Surprisingly, it worked. The cavern fell silent. Allowing Vedus to fall back with no restraint. *How was he alive?*

The last thing he remembered was one of his father's advisors rounding up him and all of his siblings and family and opening their throats. He gulped at the memory, a shiver running up his spine in fear of that painful memory.

In the blackness, he saw the shaved stone flooring. Its shaven surface was carved with great care. He found this odd, as most people mining would not give the slightest care for what the floor looked like. Yet those that carved this stone floor were meticulous and made sure to carve it in a particular way. Crimson memories permanently stained the ground, splattered against the floor with varying sizes and at varying lengths. All were originating from where he now hung from.

Fear did not settle within him. He died, what more could be done to him that was worse than that? What troubled him the most about the ordeal was the lack of being brought to Judea, the Ferryman of the Dead. He would judge the actions and deeds of who you were in life and take into consideration if a god claimed your people for an afterlife. Not once was he brought to the hands of judgement himself, but why?

His bewilderment subsided as he heard a large iron door squeal on the far side wall. Hesitation bid Vedus to not move a muscle. In the bright blinding light that shone through, he saw the silhouette of something that walked through. It lumbered on two crooked legs and hissed before stepping aside as four more reptilian monstrosities walked.

They stepped in and closed the iron door behind them. Three of them were lithe, muscled and amphibious in appearance. Rusted scalemail tightly wound around them, patches of leather holding the metal together.

The fourth was unlike anything he had seen before. Its tight leather-like scaly skin was pure white, like the first snowfall. Large fins of red webbing protruded from its forearms and crested its reptilian head. Its eyes matched the colour of the webbing, intensely and coldly inspecting the room. It was wearing silk robes etched with gold in patterns not familiar with anything he would see from his own people. Twin fangs protruded from its mouth. Bones clashed along its necklace that hung low over her neck. It stepped with a cane made of a spinal cord, rubies embedded into the eye sockets.

"It resists the Ihkar-Jharak, we have met nothing like this." One of the other reptilians said, striking Vedus as he had never heard this language before but understood what they were saying. He said nothing and listened to their conversation.

Another of the amphibious ones spoke up, "Darkness and shadows linger around it."

"Osiklim."

"Many of our Skavarn were driven mad by the darkness that cradled it."

They all spoke to the robed one, silent and cold as it laid its emotionless crimson eyes upon him. Osiklim, beyond reasoning and understanding, knew that word translated to 'Dark One'.

It finally spoke, its dialect strange, but he still understood what she was saying, "What reaction would this Osiklim have to the Ihkar-Jharak?"

Ihkar-Jharak roughly translated to 'blood-guest.' He was not sure of the usage of that word.

They all circled him now. The robed one and what he presumed to be Skavarn filled his vision a few metres in front of him. A burning sensation livened in his veins. He recognised this feeling as rage. It felt distant, however... *everything* did.

The robed figure stepped forward and drew its clawed hand to his chin. She gripped it hard and inspected him like he was some sort of animal.

It spoke in his tongue, "What powers grant you the ability to fight off vampirism?"

His cold demeanour mirrored hers as he replied, "If I did know, what good would that do you?"

It cupped his chin, claws dancing over his exposed neck as a show of certainty. Vedus was not afraid.

She said, "Power begets understanding. If we know what grants us the power to resist, then we can find a way to counteract it. If not…"

She sunk her claws into the base of his neck, blood running unto her reptilian hand. Vedus clenched his teeth as the pain flared bright hot.

She dragged her tongue along her crimson-soaked claws and finished, "Then we will remove it."

His understanding of why was beyond him, the veil over his mind was clouded much.

The dim light of the cavern was nearly snuffed out, shadows dancing across his face. His eyes flashed bright white light like the moon as he said in her dialect, "The shadows know no fear. What makes you think you can install it?"

She recoiled for a moment, the voices burst to life once more, whispering curses and ill will upon the reptilians. The Skavarn skittered in fear towards the door, not wishing to witness the maddening power of the shadows.

The robed one, however, did not scare easily and released his chin with a harsh push as she said, "We shall see."

She turned and ordered the door to open once more. They obeyed her and they quickly scampered their way out of the room and away from the crawling shadows.

When the door shut, he clenched his eyes shut and shook his head quickly to expel any further effects of the powers he used. He struggled to wrap his head around what he just did.

He was never capable of using magic before, what changed? He did not recall making a pact with some entity to gain power. Even if he did, he knew not what entity he would make a pact with to use such power.

One of his father's advisors from Sarthalas, Vena Delacroix, dabbled with the shadow's power, yet he could not recall what she would say about it despite their many conversations. The cloud over his mind frustrated him to no end.

He cursed himself as he heard the whispers mute themselves for a moment as he heard in his mind, "Well done. You will prove to be a valuable asset to my cause."

"Who are you? What do you want with me?" he barked.

For a moment, there was no answer. Then he heard her reply, "All in due time, young prince. First, you must escape your bonds."

The shadows lurched to life. The stiff darkness writhed with purpose, horrifying Vedus as he struggled against his bonds but to no avail.

They took shape, strangely enough, all taking the forms of a vaguely female shape, their hideous life now beseeching them to gather around Vedus.

Their cold hands reached out, piercing his skin and embedding a weight into his mind. He belted pain in the highest degree at their rush of secrets and knowledge.

They pressed against him, instilling memories, dreadful pain, and distant dreams of unknown suffering. Their cold hands pawed at his form. His screams echoed off the walls. He could feel his sanity slipping away. What had he done?

What dark entity was he now bound to? He detested them now, whoever it was.

He begged for the grave once more, wanting the release of death to take him. This was all too much.

The forms reached closer and now embedded themselves into him, attaching to his profaned soul. They cursed it and tore it asunder. He was slipping away, unconsciousness would take him soon.

He pleaded, "Please... please... just... just kill me."

No comfort responded. There was one form left. It sauntered up to him, pressed against him, manifesting more physically than any of them, and whispered, "You are not permitted to cease."

It climbed within him, a final blow to his blackened soul that scratched and pawed at his darkest memories.

His consciousness slipped away into the black for a single painful moment.

Chapter Five: Escaping the Arteries

Esta

Esta woke by choking on bone dust that found its way into her lungs. The ancient marrow stung as she tried to expel it from her nasal passages. The encroaching dust would not have bothered her normally, but she felt more alive than she felt dead in months.

She rolled onto her back and looked up at the intertwining bridges in the Arteries. As she lay there, she dissected what had happened to her. She died, was brought to Ebrithaera, and instructed by the God of Blood himself to kill one of his avatars and take his place. No part of that made any sense, yet it seemed to occur. Why was she chosen to be one of his avatars when she struggled to assimilate to the vampirism within?

Esta sank into the pile of bones for a moment and briefly thought of what her brother would do. As distant as the Gods were from Calisine, they sure did like to intervene more than they should. She felt out of her depth. If Ezran was present, he would probably say something along the lines of 'Stay focused and trudge on.' She gritted her teeth and clenched her eyes as she sat back up.

Stretching her arms, Esta noticed that not only colour had returned to her skin, but most of her lost muscle had too. She felt fresh and replenished, all thanks to the crawling madness of bloodlust that clung to the back of her mind.

She could feel something holding it back. It stayed at the edge, looming over her mind like some distant threat. Esta hoped it was her and not someone or something else.

There was a noticeable lack of weight in her neck. The scarab that was crushed into dust had freed her neck. Relishing the moment, she rested her hand on her neck where the scarab once was and breathed a long sigh of relief.

She drew in the profane air of the Arteries. Everything felt different with the scarab gone. Every feeling intensified a thousandfold. She felt a brimming power course through her veins, the remains of her previous meal echoing through her cursed flesh.

The half-elf slid down the bone pile and kicked up ancient dust as she found purchase on the cavern floor of the Arteries. She looked about to find Sana; they needed to talk.

Shadows danced along the mounds of bones, failed Arterians, traitor Skithik and weak prisoners used as food for the Arterians. They were all tossed to the bottom of the Arteries. Throughout the day and the night, they would periodically toss the bodies of those that failed them to the bottom of the Arteries. If they survived the plummet, they would not survive the swarms of Arterians that scuttled toward them, hungering for a decent meal.

She saw through the darkness with more clarity, thanks to the destruction of her scarab. She was grotesquely curious as to what else the scarab held back.

Esta heard Sana before seeing her. She stepped with a dark grace that Esta had not noticed before. Like a shifting shadow along the ground. Despite their need for one another, she still did not like the arrogant way she carried herself.

She stopped a few paces in front of Esta, silence thickening between them.

Esta shrugged and said, slightly annoyed by her judgemental glare, "Stop looking at me like that."

Sana tightened her gaze, "You killed me and that's all you have to say for yourself?"

The half-elf shrugged, "What are you expecting an apology?"

"Well, yes."

"And if I refuse to apologise?"

Sana stalked closer, with the scarab gone, she could feel the air warp to the dark energy that rolled off of her. She now understood why there are legends about the heirs of the name

Nailo being considered to be Lords and Ladies of the Night. Esta's throat tightened like a suffocating air that rolled off of the elf.

Sana collected her thoughts for a moment, her gaze fixed on Esta boring into her tarnished soul, as she said, "If we are to be the new Hands of Silthar, we cannot let our hatred for one another run rampant."

Esta crossed her arms and raised a defiant tone, "Just what I wanted. Hand the reins of my life from one master to another one. Delightful, just what I was asking for."

Sana clenched her jaw and spat, "Mind your wretched tongue, fledgling. You will not speak of Silthar in such a manner."

Esta dropped her arms back to her sides, her hands balling into fists, and said, "I would prefer to choose my own fate, not someone else choose it for me."

"So you would defy the will of a god?"

Esta rubbed her fingers together and replied, "Why should I have to succumb to the will of a being that does not care for my existence?"

"Esta, he cares for all that bear the blessing of—"

"I didn't ask for this!" Esta snapped. "I wasn't raised to praise the God of Blood. You were. Excuse me for not having blind obedience."

There was a pause in their conversation as Sana noticeably stiffened. Esta motioned to speak, but Sana moved a finger to her lips.

Esta stopped, her ears picking up even the slightest sound. She could hear an Arterian's laboured black heart give life for a brief moment as it fed. She listened and could hear the scuttling of insects amongst the bones. Then she heard the footsteps of claws scraping against the stone floors in the distant tunnels beyond. There were twenty of them. Esta briefly wondered why there were so many that were marching through the tunnels.

The half-elf's eyes shut as she felt the back of her neck where the scarab used to be and sighed. They knew their scarabs had died.

She pivoted to face Sana and fearfully whispered, "There's too many coming. What are we—"

Sana grabbed her arms and pulled her closer, pressing her hand against Esta's head. Burning scarlet energy burst from her palm. Esta could feel the magical energy creep into her mind.

Esta pushed her back and barked, "What in the layers of Nosgora was that!?"

Sana grumbled and said, "I was establishing a psychic link between us."

Esta tightened her glare and huffed, "You could have warned me instead of just grabbing me. What's the plan?"

"Follow me." Sana nodded her head towards the nearest bone pile.

They both crouched and hid behind it. Esta felt rage boil in her veins as she heard Sana in her mind, "Your resistance will be your downfall."

Esta turned towards Sana and said, "For the love of the Pantheon... just... focus. What's the plan?"

Sana thought for a moment, *"We would be fools not to use this time of them searching through the tunnels of the Arteries."*

"It's like a maze in here. How would we know where to go?" Esta replied. *"And how would we know the location of the Skithik."*

"If we can pick one of them off I can cast a hemomancy spell to track any that share its blood and since we are psychically linked, you would be able to know their location as well."

Esta shook her head and pursed her lips as she said, *"Yeah don't remind me..."*

"Hush. They are coming."

She heard the scraping claws against the stone floor as they marched through the tunnel that connected to the bottom of the chamber. There was grim determination in their footsteps, pure driven purpose as they rushed through the winding tunnel.

They breached the tunnel entrance, their swords and spears of bone poised and ready to strike. Like a threatening alligator, a hiss rolled from their patulous maws. They spread out from the tunnel of the opposite wall, beginning their incessant searching for them. This struck Esta as odd, as they never cared about the whereabouts of Arterians that fell before. *Why now?* She grabbed the back of her neck, the only reasoning she could find as to why.

Still crouched, Esta peaked over the side of the bone mound and watched the tunnel as the Skithik slowly began to scuttle out of the shadows beyond the tunnel.

Esta said, "Alright, we'll wait for them to come over here and when the moment is right, we will bring one down."

She waited for a moment for a reply, but only the captured wind of the Arteries answered her.

"Sana? Sana!"

She turned around and saw that Sana was gone. Her blood boiled as she frantically searched the chamber for her.

Looking about, she scanned the pit of bones and saw no trace of her. Where could she have gone? Esta's frustration reached its peak, her hands crushing a bone she leaned her hands against.

Refocusing on the tunnel, the last of the Skithik came through and Esta watched as a shadow above the tunnel moved. It was formless and drifted along the surface of the stone like a spectre.

It moved across the far side wall of the chamber and ducked behind a bone pile.

Esta waited once more, the rage subsiding for a few moments as she whispered to herself.

"What in the Pantheon's name is she doing now?"

She already hated having to work with Sana. If they were supposed to be in the hands of Silthar, then why did it only feel like Esta was pushing to have them work as a team? It angered her to no end.

A Skithik moved past the bone pile the shadow hid behind. Spear raised, ready to impale any that dared to ambush it.

It was not fast enough as the shadow grabbed him, pulled him behind the pile, and disappeared.

Esta waited patiently. The rage dimmed but lingered as she anticipated them both to be next to her.

Esta said, "Dinner for two?"

Sana ignored her comment and dropped the lifeless frame of the Skithik, fresh blood dripping from her mouth and a gash along its neck. She wiped her mouth and said, "Alright, now I just need a moment to cast the spell."

The half-elf bore her sight through Sana, who only gave her a disapproving glare.

"What?"

Esta shrugged her shoulders as she grabbed the spear in the stiffened Skithik's claws. She tested its weight and said, "Oh, you know, the usual. Just on the run from those that kept me as their indentured servant and psychically connected to a sociopath."

"I would be more inclined to keep you informed if you didn't blatantly label me as suffering from madness."

"Gods above, we have Skithik searching for us. We don't have time for this. We can argue about religion and ethics when we don't have an entire nation of bloodsucking lizards on our heels."

Sana rolled her eyes as she began her spell.

Esta cursed to herself and peered over the edge of the bone pile. This new role of being a Hand of Silthar was most certainly going to be interesting.

Chapter Six: From Whence Shadows Came

Sana

Their blood ran long, their ancestry went on for centuries before the official establishment of the elves on Calisine. Sana knew about this but to see it before her eyes was remarkable. A people with nearly as long and complicated a history as the Dwarves, whom they sided with in the Illithaun War. What was most interesting was the fact that what they used as vampirism was not to be compared to the blessing that was granted by Silthar. Rather than acting as a bestowment of magical abilities, the Skithik vampirism acted as more of a symbiotic ailment.

Crawling back into her mind, the whispers and prayers from her bloodline roused once more. She heard them across so many kilometres. Her temples drummed with pain and breathing slowly. She dimmed the voices that crawled into her mind. She reached out to her bloodline to replenish some of her lost strength. There was a wall in place. Perhaps her version of the reconditioning prevented her from connecting to her bloodline. These lizards were smart. They couldn't sever the connection, not without killing Sana, but they could impede it somehow. Sana stored this problem away for a later date.

Sana attempted to absorb some of the magical energy, refilling the font of magic that resided within her. It refused.

While auguring, she communicated with the magical energy to understand why. As she pressed the issue, forcing the magical energy within, a sting erupted on the back of her neck. The scarab's corruptive nature was lingering within her. She would need to remedy this. For now, she would have to rely on the magic of the dead.

As she toiled with the magical energy, reading and auguring the energy, she looked to her newly acquired companion. Esta tested the weight of the spear that the Skithik once held, seeming to find it satisfactory. It was longer than the typical spear in the hands of Esta, but she seemed to pay no mind to that. She grabbed the curved shortsword that was sheathed on its belt, then the rusty scale mail, fitting it as tightly as she could. It was large when she put it on, but it was better to have that than nothing at all. Sana saw a familiarity brighten in her scarlet-hued eyes. She was eager to feel the weight of a weapon once more.

Esta peered over the bone pile at the roaming Skithik.

"Find anything?"

Sana slowly closed her hand and the magical energy slowly evaporated with the motion. She pushed out a long sigh and replied, "Prince Vedus Ostrogoth is being held in a separate chamber in the Arteries. They are torturing him to find a way to get past his immunity to vampirism."

"Is such a thing possible?" Esta asked, leaning her shoulder against the bone pile with her spear at the ready.

Sana answered, "It's beyond their understanding. It's the most advanced spellwork that I have seen. To form more advanced forms of magic, the practitioner has to combine complementary elements. A heavily trained wizard might be capable of this, but certainly not a human prince."

Esta mused, "Could this hypothetical wizard impart that immunity onto another?"

Sana shook her head, "Not from the mortal plane."

Esta bore a worried expression, though it took a minute or two for Sana to notice. To be immune to such powerful dark magic was beyond even the complex magics of the Pantheon itself. Only one division of magic had even an inkling of such complexity, the Void Pantheon. Though it took tremendous effort for those entities to interact with the material plane, it was the only option she could conceive.

Sana stood up and joined Esta's side as they studied the movements of the Skithik together. Only five remained in the pit, the other fifteen had run back through the tunnels to find them. They hissed and barked orders at each other. Due to studying their nature from their blood, she understood the basics of their language. Now able to discern its writing, but not speak it.

Esta said, "Alright, can we form an actual plan? I don't want to gather the attention of any more Skithik."

Sana rolled her eyes, deciding to ignore the comment, "We need to either distract or dispatch these Skithik. The others are in higher tunnels. We need not worry about them for now."

Esta nodded, "They know these tunnels more than we do. They have that advantage. I say we make quick work of these Skithik on our tails, get our prince, and get the hell out of here."

She paused, drinking in the weight of her spear. There was an eagerness in her eyes, a yearning for bloodshed. She gave a sinister smile and said, "I've been waiting a long time for this."

Sana was taken aback by her sadistic look, but most soldiers yearned for the battlefield once more. The Song of

War rages on, as they say. For some, Esta included, war was all they knew.

She moved her hand behind her and drew upon the magical energy of the deceased Skithik's blood and she said as she collected the blood in a telekinetic grip, "Then follow my lead."

She opened her palm to the air. The blood congealed and writhed with purpose. Forming into a small three-foot-sized dart, sharpened to a deadly point.

She sprung out from behind the bone pile and chose her targets.

Two were lined next to each other, sifting through one of the bone piles, not ten metres out. Little did they know, their search would be fruitless.

She willed the blood dart and it went sailing through the air at a blinding speed, piercing through scale, neck, and bone. Piercing through one and continuing its trail, embedding itself in the other. They slumped to the ground, their lives snuffed out from the material plane.

Esta charged the other three and Sana watched with care as she charged them. She dodged and parried their blows with relative ease. Esta was a seasoned warrior from countless battles and skirmishes.

One peeled off and charged toward Sana, snarling with unbridled fury and its two hand axes ready to hack into her flesh.

She drew on the magical energy of the fleeing spirits of the two Skithik she had killed. Enough for a handful of spells. It had to be enough.

The Skithik guard unleashed a flurry of blows, each blocked by a solidified crimson force field that she brought into existence. Having his mighty attacks shielded caused great anger to rise within the Skithik.

She dodged one of the blows and blinked a horizontal blade of scarlet energy that passed through the top of its chest. The blade stopped midway down its torso. Not yet dead and reeling from the pain, one of its axes sliced her arm. A narrow cut that stung as if someone dipped it into a forge. She looked as it shimmered in the lowlight of the Arteries. Her eyes widened. *Of course*, it was silver.

Grunting at the pain, she used the last of the mortal energies to punch her hand in the air, palm out and send out a ray of scarlet energy striking the Skithik's face. It seared the flesh from its skull, a mortifying cry of pain escaping from the Skithik guard as it crumbled to the ground.

Sana had little time to recover, the disparate feeling of not using her magical reserves was gruelling and she already felt mental fatigue begin to plant its roots. She drew on the magical energy of its spirit as it fell lifeless to the ground. Her breath caught in her throat, straining against the magical resistance.

Whipping her head, she found Esta engaged with two of the Skithik guard.

They were seemingly equal in strength one another, yet Esta was smaller and had agility on her side. She kept up with deflecting and parrying strikes from each of them. One swung from high with a powerful downward slash, colliding with her shortsword. However, she was at a slight disadvantage due to wielding both a spear and a shortsword.

She pressed onward, thrusting her spear towards one of the Skithik guards. It parried the strikes but backpedalled.

Flicking her wrist, she summoned a portion of the lingering magical energy from the dead Skithik and the air in her palm warped, distorting to the necrotic energy that writhed and thrashed with unnatural ferocity.

She propelled the energy forward. It was a simple spell, but she doubted the Skithik guard was trained to shield themselves from magical attacks. Bursting forth, it collided with the Skithik guard that approached Esta from behind, weapon poised to strike. As it roared, the necrotic energy entered its gaped maw and burst with enough force to liquefy its skin, bone, and flesh.

Struck with horror, Esta took the opening and plunged her spear deep into the Skithik's sternum. Wrenching it deep into its hardened flesh, dark red blood coated her hands and the haft of her spear, choking on its words as the life drained from its eyes.

Esta sheathed her sword and nodded towards the far door and said, "Let's find Prince Vedus and get out of here."

***

Their night-blessed footsteps made almost no noise as they rushed through the tunnels of the Arteries. They did not scramble. The clairvoyant spell that Sana cast illuminated their path and assured their steps. Her mind strained against her liberal use of magic but they had no other way of knowing where to find the wayward prince.

Esta said, "You still with me?"

Sana clenched her eyes shut against the rising pain in her mind as she replied, "I'll be fine."

With the aid of the spell, it was as if recalling a distant memory. Sana always found it interesting how much information could be gained from blood. History bleeds from all, as the Crimson Order would say. Zealots that Sana found to be obsessed with the information stored in the blood. They prided themselves on having samples from nearly every royal family, previously alive or still alive and were constantly trying to find ways to gain more information from the blood. Sana held no such gruesome fascination with the blood, but she was always spellbound at how much was kept within the crimson life essence.

They came to a split, then halted.

They could sense them coming from the left pathway. They were charging fast.

Sana said, "They found our victims."

Esta pressed to the right and motioned for Sana to follow, "Then let's not wait and see what they have to say to us."

They charged through the dark and wound their way to a place that they pulled from one of the Skithik. They were deeply afraid. They referred to Vedus as Osiklim which roughly translated to, from her very limited knowledge of the language, 'Dark One'.

Sana was not easily scared, but if something had such a sadistic creature scared, then that was more than enough proof for her to approach with caution.

They came to a dead end but a large solid iron door that seemed to have no reason to be there. Age had barely touched the smooth metal surface. Esta inspected and moved to open it.

Sana reached out and said, "Wait."

"What?"

"I think we should be careful."

Esta raised an eyebrow, "What? Are you scared to meet your first human? Because they are more afraid of you than you are—"

"No, not that. Something wasn't right about the spellwork I saw."

Esta shrugged, "We need him and the Skithik are hunting us down. We don't have the time."

Curling her lip in frustration, she said, "Fine."

Esta stepped to the side of the door, spear raised, the dull glimmer still shining in the darkness.

The half-elf nodded her approval to open the door.

Sana grabbed two handles and shifted them in opposite positions that released bolts, squealing the hinges to life. A great force was needed to open the doors, luckily, she held strength from her blessing from Silthar.

She pushed the large metal door open, and from the air that wafted into her nostrils, Sana knew the dark powers that ruminated in the darkness. It was not the sulphurous air of a demonic presence. It was the musty putrescence of a room haunted by the dead. Ancient and primal, the air thrummed with the lingering magic of shadows. It was *her*.

The cavern room was perhaps three metres in diametre, the floor and ceiling damp with ancient dew, telling Sana that it once held water. In the centre of the chamber was a table that stood upright upon the surface and was the unconscious form of Prince Vedus.

She knew him fairly well from the dealings that the elves had with him when his family was still in power before the Night of Black Swords. She saw the wound around his neck, the scar of when he was killed. His skin was pale, and she would have thought him dead but sensed something that gave him life. Something familiar but foreign.

As she stepped through the threshold, Esta said, "Huh, I thought he'd be dead."

Sana replied, still inspecting the former prince of Aebolon, "He should be."

"Necromancy?"

"No, that's what's strange; it's not a spell."

Sana was a metre or so away from Vedus as she continued, "It's some sort of dark essence that mimics the spirit."

Esta pushed past Sana and said, sword raised, keeping her eyes on the door, "We can talk about it later."

Sana summoned another small portion of magic and willed the shackles free.

Vedus grunted as Esta chopped the other binding free.

They both caught him as he slowly awakened. Esta said, "Woah, easy there. We need you on your feet."

He grunted and said, "Huh… what… *who* are you? Why are you here?"

Sana said in an even tone, trying her best to soothe him and not agitate him in some way, "We can explain that later. Right now, all you need to know is we are here to save you and take you to safety."

He looked over at Sana and with a narrow brow and dark, almost black, brown eyes. "Why should I trust you?"

Esta piped up and said, as the tunnels lit up with cries and shouts of promised pain, "Because we can promise you that we're easier to deal with than the ones that brought you here in the first place."

Vedus conceded, "Very well."

They let him go. He was woozy but remained on his feet. Most human princes knew how to fight. Esta hoped Vedus was one such a prince.

The cries grew louder and Sana said, "We have no time to waste."

Chapter Seven: Shadow and Blood

Esta

Though they stepped into the open sands of Urstron, they could feel the nipping jaws of the Skithik on their heels. They pressed on through the night, and into the morning, the sun lingered upon Esta's skin. She felt its rays oppressively bear down upon her. Everything that she had gained from her feeding, including her supernatural strength, was nullified because of the sun.

Esta looked over to Sana, *"You have any magical reserves left?"*

Sana's breaths were heavy as she replied, *"Enough to keep them at bay, I'd be more comfortable if it were night, but I have enough to not die."*

"That's comforting to know, I suppose."

Vedus kept up with them. His strength seemed to have returned to him, yet the same could not be said about his colour. Valamer's ilk all bore soft jawlines and the demure features befitting a noble. Though the blood of ancient kings flowed through their veins, it showed with little complexity. His hair was ragged and whipped against him as they charged through the sands. His eyes harboured a great deal of pain and though she knew little in the ways of magic, there was a prominent aura that rolled off of him. Every part of her told her to cast him away and leave him to die. There was evil that made its home within him, but not of his own. Vedus was quite the anomaly.

Esta turned back and saw a warband of the Skithik charging through the sands on their heels. Swords, spears, and axes drawn to pierce their flesh. Due to their small size and head start, they were considerably ahead of them, but that would not be enough to stop the reptilian overlords.

Their feet touched not sand but soaking wet moors. Desert made its way into a dark and sinister-looking swamp. Dead trees breached the surface of the moors like fingers breaching the ground just before rising from the grave. Like dark green veils, the leaves of the trees clung and billowed in the wispy air that danced along their skin.

They trudged through the swamp, and Esta looked at Sana, "They are going to keep following us unless we do something about them."

Sana whipped her head to Esta, "Like what? Neither of us has the strength to take on an entire warband."

Esta shrugged, stepping long through the knee-deep waters of the swamp, "Anything is better than right now.

Once they reach the swamp, they will gain on us much faster."

"Can we distract them?" Vedus asked.

"They lost two of their Arterians and one of their prized prisoners. I don't think there's a way to distract them, at least not for very long." Esta gagged at the noxious and thick air of the moors, which was suffocating her senses.

There was no time to pause. Breaching the top of the nearest dune, five Skithik burst forth with weapons drawn. They held bows and began to fire upon the small band of rebels.

Esta and Vedus ducked and weaved through the hail of arrows back towards the sands. Sana deflected and blocked with summon shields of bright red magical energy. Every arrow she blocked was harder than the last. Her limbs trembled with exhaustion.

The half-elf handed her shortsword over to the prince, and he tested the weight. Esta said, "Don't get captured."

Vedus replied, flinching as an arrow grazed the top of their cover, "I didn't plan on it."

Weaving magical energy in her hands and speaking a brief arcane word, Sana laid her hands down, thumbs touching and fingers splayed out. The half-elf knew the spell she was casting and braced herself.

Esta felt the heat before the dune erupted in flames. Jets of flame burst forth with reckless abandon at three of them. Turning the sand to glass and flesh to char as the tongues of flame lapped against them. Sana stumbled as her spell finished, collapsing to her knees.

Esta rushed to Sana and clapped a hand on her shoulder and said, "Stay with me, Sana."

Her eyes almost rolled back into her head as she struggled not to succumb to magical exhaustion.

Esta shook her slightly with no response. She readied her spear.

She connected blows with one. It snarled and hissed at the former Arterian. She could feel the strength that it carried as they exchanged strikes.

She tested the capabilities with the strikes of her spear, keeping Sana in her peripheral and distancing the Skithik away from her. He was younger in terms of the Skithik, but he knew his way around a blade. Esta noted that most of the Skithik did, despite their limited use of the sword.

In an overhead strike, its eyes grew wild and it unleashed an oppressive flurry of strikes. She risked breaking her spear if she parried those strikes with it. She narrowly dodged and weaved through the unrelenting assault.

Tucking and rolling back, she burst to her feet as it raised its bone sword and poised itself, ready to unleash another flurry of attacks.

Before the strike came down, Esta kicked up sand into the Skithik's eyes. It cried out and lost its will to unleash its attacks.

Esta, quick as lightning, plunged her spear deep into the lizard's neck.

She wrenched the spear out again and drove it through the Skithik's exposed navel. A pathetic cry erupted from the Skithik.

The half-elf looked up and saw Vedus dispatch his Skithik. He had the lizard on its knees, gliding his blade over the Skithik's neck. Blood drenched the sands at their feet.

Sana rose to her feet as if a great weight bore down on her. She motioned with her hand and willed the freshly spilled blood to take the form of a two-metre-long lance. It sailed through the air and impaled the three singed Skithik guard. They were perfectly lined up in front of her as she willed the spear through all three of them. Impressive as it was, Sana collapsed onto the sands.

Vedus donned scale mail from the lithe creature he had just killed. Quickly tightening the straps.

Esta's eyes widened as she saw a hulking monstrosity charging towards them. She leaped to Vedus and tackled him to the ground, narrowly dodging the charging force.

It was massive, taller than any Skithik they had faced so far. Its scales were a pale white and wore a plate of polished gold that not a single grain of sand dared to tarnish. In its tight grip was a longsword of golden steel that shimmered and blinded in the rays of the sun. Though gold in appearance, Esta squinted her eyes at the glimmering silver it was truly made of. It was a spectacle to behold, but Esta raised her spear, poised to strike.

The beast raised its sword and deflected each blow from Vedus and Esta as they both unleashed their own flurries.

It parried their attacks with ease, taking in their fighting styles and studying their moves. This was not a simple Skithik guard, this was a well-trained warrior of the lizard overlords. She had never seen any that belonged to the upper class of the Visceran.

It found an opening as it simultaneously deflected one of Esta's and Vedus's attacks. It stepped back to avoid one of Vedus's attacks. Using the opening, it collided a clawed fist into the scale mail that Vedus had just acquired. Its claws did not find flesh, but it gripped the breastplate of rusted steel and pulled Vedus closer, forcing the prince to his knees.

Its eyes glowed with unfettered rage as it raised its sword towards Esta as she lost her footing.

Sword raised and pointed towards her. Its eyes and the ruby in its guard glowed with shimmering scarlet energy.

The air rippled and a shockwave burst forth from the golden blade of the Visceran warrior.

Esta narrowly dodged the wave of energy, but her feet could not grip the ground as she slid further down the dune.

Fear gripped her voice as she saw the Visceran warrior lift its sword and plunge into the awaiting prince.

Vedus's sword caught the guard as the sword was centimetres from his neck.

They struggled there for a moment, contesting their strength. The Visceran warrior was a vampire, such as Sana and Esta. He did not flinch or waver as he forced his strength with ease. Vedus, on the other hand, struggled to keep the sword at bay.

With little time, Esta reversed her spear and raised it like a javelin. Before she let it loose, she saw an ethereal shadow energy bleed from Vedus' eyes. She heard shadows whisper as she looked at the prince.

The Visceran warrior's shadow was brought to life, rising from the still existence against the crawling dune.

The shadow poised its sword and pierced through armour and flesh. However, it did not falter and continued on its attack. This proved that the Visceran warrior was born and bred for combat, the promise of pain and death in its cold, orange-tinted eyes.

Sana shambily charged up the dune, wreathed in the lost scarlet essence of life, reaching her palms out and willed to existence a shockwave similar to the one the Visceran cast not too long ago.

It batted her aside as it absorbed the attack.

Esta launched her spear at the Visceran with all of her might and watched as it sailed through the air. It pierced deep into the flesh of the Visceran and howled and hissed as the silver-tipped spear plunged deep within its flesh. It cried out but continued with its attack, causing Esta to charge the brute.

Another strike from the livened shadow, a horizontal strike that stole more mortal essence from the Visceran warrior. Esta could not tackle the brute but instead weaved her arms around the sword arm of the Visceran warrior. She pulled and strained against the strength as Vedus shook, his muscles nearly giving out.

Lifting its blade, Vedus lost grip on his weapon. The Visceran warrior tossed him over the side of the dune. The brute shook against Esta as she clung to the golden warrior of the Skithik.

Sana unleashed a dart of solidified blood. The warrior twisted around and used Esta to absorb the attack. The dart plunged into her back, piercing through her armour and flesh. Esta screamed in pain as the warm sting of the dart's entry was unlike any physical pain she had endured before.

She lost her strength, plummeting to the sandy ground and collapsing to her knees. She watched as Sana unleashed another dart but to no avail as the Visceran warrior dispelled the dart as it found purchase on his awaiting palm. Spent, Sana collapsed once more.

It raised its sword, ready to decapitate Esta. In one fleeting moment, the half-elf felt her spirit flinch as the Visceran stood poised to take her life.

The Visceran growled in common as it said, "Die now, wretch."

Esta closed her eyes, waiting for her hideous end.

She heard the sound of steel finding flesh and opened her eyes when she realised it was not her own.

She saw steel breaching through the solar plexus of the brute, where no gold armour protected its soft awaiting flesh. The wounded half-elf saw Vedus, drenched in blood and sweat. His teeth bared in anger. The prince growled, "Not today, cold-blooded bastard."

Blood tarnished the blade. Esta pulled the dart from her back and grunted against the pain as it hurt just as bad when it found her flesh, holding back tears as she did so. She had to remove a few arrows from herself many times, but it had no comparison to the white-hot pain that welled in her back.

The brute lost grip of its sword and fell to his knees. Vedus wrenched his sword free and opened the Visceran's wide neck.

Esta stood up, gripping the handle of the golden sword, and spat at the lizard warrior.

Vedus and Esta reversed their blades and plunged them into the shoulders of the Visceran warrior. Hilting their blades, their swords peaked from the hips of the warrior.

They all wrenched their swords from the Visceran warrior, breaths of relief and tiredness released from all of them as they exchanged looks.

Esta nodded to Vedus and said, "Thank you. Name's Esta, by the way."

Vedus breathed heavily and said, "Vedus Ostrogoth and thank you for rescuing me."

She then looked to Sana, who was unresponsive as she lay in the sand. She had not died, but she would need to rest to recover.

Esta rolled her shoulder and said, "I am so tired of these lizards."

Hoisting Sana onto her shoulders, they entered the moors once more. Esta saw many conflicts rise and fall throughout her aged life. She knew that their journey to uproot these Skithik was only just beginning.

Chapter Eight: Ancient Blood

The shell of rusted iron that wrapped around Vedus did little to protect him with what remained after their fight with the Visceran warrior. His muscles still ached from the battle.

They salvaged what they could off of the fallen warrior. There was enough leather to fashion under armour which did well to put both him and Esta at ease, who fashioned crude leather armour over her unconscious companion. They shared pieces of armour that fit, the gold plates that fit their size. She fashioned his backplate into a makeshift shield. He took up the golden sword that the warrior wielded, fitting in his hands more as a greatsword than a longsword as he wielded it. They did not know if it was because the armour was imprinted by the warrior, but the metal had begun to degrade and tarnish.

Her eyes told many stories of war and death, she was a child of Rath and they received more attention in recent times. Vedus could not help but wonder where his country stood after his death. War likely ravaged the long peace of the Eternium and only recently was the Elves and Dwarves able to reconcile the bad blood between them after the Incursion of the Sons of Arnthor. The Dwarves would stand against his father's general. They are of resilient stock and were the first empire established on Ketos.

Esta motioned for them to stop and said, "There is a dry spot over here. We can rest there."

Esta dropped her companion.

"Will she be okay?"

Esta cracked her neck and said, stretching her arms, "Yeah, she'll be fine. Just magical exhaustion."

Vedus saw the marking on Esta's exposed shoulder. It was one of the ancestral marks of the half-elven families. If Vedus's cloudy mind was correct, she was one of the Desidarius clan.

They fashioned makeshift bed rolls from the scales from the Skithik as well, rolling them out and forming a circle around a fire. Vedus sat upon his bedroll and looked out into the darkness. He looked through the rows of dead trees and could vaguely make out what looked to be a town. From this distance, he could see the buildings were on stilts so as to not sink into the swamps. Any further details were as murky as the swamp waters that threatened to swallow the lands.

Esta rested her blade on her lap and began to clean the blade of blood and asked, "So, can we talk about the magic you used when we fought the Visceran?"

The shadows murmured at the mention of their power, Vedus closed his eyes, trying to ignore them and said, "I didn't cast that spell."

Esta seemed unconvinced, "I'm not well versed when it comes to magic, but I know pact magic when I see it."

This struck Vedus as odd. How would a half-elf know about pact magic? Her people had no deities that claimed them as their children, not to mention the sheltered nature of the Rathians. But he decided to leave that matter alone and said, "I'm sorry, but I have no more information for you. I still can't think clearly."

The half-elf nodded. The only sound being the fire that Vedus tried to make and Esta's rustling as she cleaned her sword and hands.

The prince stared at Esta's mark on her shoulder and said, "You're from the Desidarius clan?"

Esta paused and looked at Vedus with fury behind her scarlet irises, "Yes. And I would prefer not to talk about my family. We left on... *ill terms*. And yes, not even my brother is looked upon fondly in my family's eyes anymore."

As she returned to her cleaning, Vedus said as he got the fire going, "Your brother being Ezran?"

Esta licked her lips in agitation and said, "The same. We're twins."

Vedus nodded and stared at the fire for some time. He thought of his family's hearth, the large mantelpiece that bore the paintings of all the previous rulers of Mildoron and Aebolon proper. He could almost see the sprawling wheat fields as Spring rolled across the countryside. Vedus fought back the tears as he clung to that feeling, even as the whispers of the shadows crawled back to him. The wisps of smoke formed shapes and forced Vedus to blink and force the faces that he saw to bury deep into his mind.

She finished her cleaning and rolled her shoulders as she added, "You have no questions?"

Vedus shook his head and said, "About?"

Esta waved her hand as she grabbed a stick and prodded the fire, "Usually, folk bend over backwards to hear something new about him."

Vedus paused for a moment and mused to his half-elf rescuer, "No. He was the advisor to my father for some time. I know of his deeds well."

He gave a half-hearted smile and said, "And I know the effect that a sibling's shadow can have."

Years of clawing his way to become heir to the throne ran through his mind. He did not hate his siblings, nor did he suspect they hated him. He wished he could tell them now how much they meant to him. Their fearful expressions were all he could think of now.

Coming out of his reverie, Vedus saw a small smirk that perhaps silently thanked him for understanding her plight. She said, "Well, I'm gathering that you might be quite starving. I'll return with some food."

Vedus beat back his pleading as he said, "Perhaps it would be best to wait until your companion awoke?"

Esta nodded and sat back down.

In their conversation's pause, Vedus looked past the belt of trees that wrapped around their clearing and into the sky. The stars shone brightly, twinkling against distant glowing space dust that churned and boiled. For a brief and wonderful moment, he forgot all of the woes that plagued his damaged mind. The mists cleared and he recalled when he and his mother would gaze up and she would tell him about the constellations and their stories.

The prince rushed back to reality as he asked, "What do you want with me?"

Esta shrugged her shoulders, "Why do you assume that we need you? Perhaps we saw you being carried into the Arteries, found pity, and when we sprung our escape, we decided to take you with us."

Vedus picked at the issue again, digging deeper, "No. You knew me by name and told me that you would give an explanation as to why you freed me. Before we continue, I want to know the reason."

Esta sighed and said, "Fine, the truth is we have no clue as to why we need you. We just know what we need from you."

"How can you know that you need me when you don't even know the reason why? You're either a liar or your logic is supremely flawed."

Esta jumped to her feet and pointed her blade to Vedus's throat, "Do not tarnish the honour of my name by accusing me of being a liar. You asked for the truth and I gave it. Why do you insist on making me angry?"

As she huffed, he could not help but see her protruding canines and feel a mote of fear well up within him. She must have noticed as she composed herself and lowered her blade. He said, "I apologise, I didn't mean to offend you or your family. I'm just confused."

Esta plopped back down, sheathing her sword and sighed, "Yeah... me too."

Vedus looked and saw Esta's companion groaning awake.

Esta smiled as she said, "Welcome back to the land of the living."

She slowly sat up and pressed her fingers against her head and said, "By the Gods, don't let me do that again."

Vedus leaned over and outstretched his hand. She flinched, eyes wide in horror and looked to Esta, who patted the air as she sifted the ashes of the fire.

Hesitantly, she clasped her hand around his, "Vedus Ostrogoth."

She replied after a cough, "Sana Nailo."

Vedus chuckled slightly, garnering the attention of both of them and responded to their looks of confusion, "The Nailos and the Desidarius seem to be intertwined. Ezran met with Silas in Mildoron a few weeks before…"

His voice trailed off as he pawed his neck.

Sana leaned in, desperation in her eyes, "He was in the capitol before the Night of Black Swords? Alive?"

Vedus nodded, "Who is he to you?"

Sana pursed her lips and responded, "He is my father."

Esta and Sana exchanged looks, their expressions shifting from conversational, to an argument, to conversational again.

Esta grabbed her spear and trudged off without a word.

Sana scooted closer to him and the fire. Vedus asked, "What was that all about?"

She replied, "Nothing concerning. I asked if she could get me some water while she went off hunting."

He nodded. "Ah, I see."

Vedus plied for information from her as he asked, "So, about that explanation as to why you both need me?"

"I'm sorry, Prince Vedus, but I do not have the answer for that. I have been praying to Silthar as to why but—"

Vedus burst to his feet and said with fear in his voice, "Silthar? You're a worshipper of the Great Betrayer? You plan to sacrifice me to him, sanctify my blood and drink it to gain his blessing!"

Sana chuckled and said, "If you were our sacrifice, then why do we have you untied and are willing to feed you and arm you? If you were our sacrifice—"

She paused, flashing her sharpened teeth and a sinister glee in her eyes as she said, "— I would have already partaken."

Vedus calmed for a moment, conceding to her logic, and sat back down.

Sana crossed her legs as she said, "So, Prince Vedus, tell me how you yet live?"

Pulling the memory from the dark nebulous cloud that hung over his mind, he replied, "I don't know. All that I know is whatever brought me back to life is not the most benevolent."

"I don't know for sure, but you seem to have garnered the attention of the Shadow Queen."

Vedus gulped.

The shadows roared awake at the mere sound of their queen's name. They praised her and those shadow figures that implanted themselves into him.

He shook the memories away and said, "How? Why?"

"The intentions of the Temptress Queen are hard to place. Her webs weave through centuries and the fruition of those plans might not come to roost for centuries after their beginning. You are her pawn. She preys upon those that fall under her gaze. Any servant is manipulated into breaking their spirit and doing disgusting and deplorable things before her need for them is done. Then she tosses them aside."

"Noted!"

Sana chuckled to herself and said, "I'm sorry to worry you, but like I said, her need for you likely stretches beyond your mortal coil. Such seems to be the ways of the Void Pantheon."

"You know much about the gods. Are you a cleric of the Pantheon?"

"Oh no, my father would interact with them often and would tell me about their plans and how they act."

"Interact?"

"Yes, my father is Silas Nailo, after all."

Vedus looked off towards where Esta stormed off and said, "Indeed he is."

The twin of the most prominent warrior and protector of the Eternium and the daughter of the Nine-Slayer himself. Whatever the plans were for him, certainly: their need for him will undoubtedly be great and terrifying. He lost his appetite, not for food but for information, and silently stared into the crackling flames.

Chapter Nine: Heart of the Lost

Esta hoped their prince liked rabbits. She had already caught five of them, and as she hunted, Esta spotted a nearby village. The village was a few thousand years old, with not a soul kicking up dust from the village in aeons. Mould and mildew overtook most of the ruined wooden structures. Moss covered the rest.

She neared the edge of the moors when she heard the most intoxicating sound she had ever heard, a heartbeat.

Thump-thump… thump-thump…

She stopped in her tracks; Esta looked over to the dunes. Her fangs extended, a primal urge overtaking her. She took a few steps towards the sound and then used what reservations she could muster to stop.

Thump-thump… thump-thump…

She pressed a hand to her head and clenched her eyes shut as she said to herself, "No… no… not here… not now… I can't."

Thump-thump… thump-thump…

She opened her eyes and found herself on the dunes of Urstron; the heartbeat was louder in her ears. Her hands trembled as she said, "No, I'm stronger than this…I am…"

Esta saw her. A lone woman, meandering across the sands. Broken. Looking around, breathing heavily and darting her head to see if anything or anyone was following her. Her ragged clothing was stained red, wounds along her chest and arms flowed freely. Esta stared directly at the crimson flow that stained the sands. On the wind, the sweet scent of her blood filled her nose. She was wounded and would surely perish in the dunes with her wounds; who would know? Who would miss her? She was probably an escaped slave from Ardarian that had not yet turned.

Thump-thump… thump-thump…

Esta cast the rabbit carcasses away and fell to her knees in the sand. Her breaths escaped her laboriously, and she shook as the primal hunger for blood overtook her thoughts.

In her mind, she heard the sound of Ezran's voice, *"Do it. You're a monster anyway."*

Esta's trembling stopped for a moment as she said to herself, "Ezran? No… I'm not—"

"You bring shame to our… My family. You're nothing but a black stain. Forgotten."

All thoughts ceased as she slowly stalked down the dune, tears rolling down her cheeks. Esta was a few yards away. The woman's heartbeat resounded throughout all of Esta, and it willed her forward. She rushed behind the wandering woman. Fangs extended, and Esta lost all control.

Thump-thump… thump…

A sickening pierce awoke the silence of the sands—hand cupping the woman's mouth to silence her cries of pain and horror. Esta's hand moved over the open wound on her left arm. *The crimson, oh the crimson.*

The woman tried to resist with all her might, but no hope was left. Her hands slapped against Esta's titanic grip. They slowed as Esta drained the life from her until no resistance remained.

Relishing all till the last drop, Esta retracted her fangs and looked at the now-dead woman.

Her hair matched the black night sky. Her skin was now pale and devoid of life. Esta's hands were stained with the last of her mortal essence. Esta saw her reflection in the glossy lifeless eyes of the woman.

Esta knelt in the crimson-stained sands and felt tears form in her eyes as she cradled the woman's body. All relishment faded.

***

Esta returned with her trappings, skinned them, dressed them, and cooked Vedus's meal. Her hands and mouth were cleaned of her dreadful act.

Wordlessly, Esta presented Vedus his meal. His eyes bore a look of ignorant sympathy as she sat back down.

He blinked and shook his head as he began to eat his meal, continuing his statement from their previous conversation, "As I was saying: my father anticipated a conflict. He might not have been military-minded, but he knew the political state well enough to see this."

Sana nodded pensively, "The Song of War rages on… when we return, I wonder if there will be an Eternium left."

War was a constant danger. Conflict arose between nations as quickly as the wind would blow.

"You're a monster anyways…" Esta buried her brother's words, grabbed a piece of flint from the Skithik provisions they took, and said as she began to sharpen her sword, "No one can say for certain… if the Night of Black Swords was any indication, this conflict is far from over."

Finishing half of his meal, Vedus asked, "How long have you both been away from Ketos?"

Esta stopped her sharpening briefly, "Four years."

"Six and a half." Sana replied.

Esta looked at Sana as the half-elf continued her sharpening.

"What happened during the scouting?"

There was no pause in her actions as Esta replied, *"Nothing...."*

Sana sighed, using the break of conversation to commune with her reserves of arcane. Though Esta's knowledge of the arcane arts was limited, she had seen enough mages in her time to know when they were refilling their magical reserves. Whether born with magical reserves or using some ritual to bind oneself to the leylines of magic, all had to rekindle their arcane reserves.

Esta brushed her thumb over the edge of her blade, satisfied with her work. As she sheathed her sword, Vedus motioned to say something as he finished his first rabbit. His words died in his throat, Esta assumed he was going to ask if the half-elves had any stake in the current conflict on Ketos. Then he likely remembered Esta's exile and ceased.

Vedus looked to the sky and said, "If it is all the same to you two, I will retire for the night."

As Vedus readied for a night's sleep, Esta stood and walked away from the campfire. She could still hear her heartbeat.

She sat upon a fallen tree and looked at the dunes and the distant mountains. Desperately, she thought back to her time growing up in Rath to ease her mind from her most recent feeding.

"Sleep well, Vedus. We leave at dawn's break." Sana said as she walked over to Esta. She had to have known what had transpired. Esta could see it in her eyes.

Sana sat down, a metre next to her, staring off into the night sky. She took in a sharp breath before saying, "Part of becoming a member of the council of blood we have to start our bloodline. The strength of vampires comes not from the individual but from those that stand with us. I started my bloodline on Ketos, a duke from Aebolon. Lord Alcaste. He was who I saw the ideals of my bloodline to be. Strong. Loyal. Merciful. With him at my side, we could accomplish great things. I prepared him for the trials he would face ahead.

"I made sure to teach him how to control the unbridled passions, the hunger, and the boundless power. I thought I had prepared him for what was to come. But even I couldn't prepare for how the blessing would corrupt him. It fed his inhibitions and bred a merciful ruler into a tyrant. It overtook him. I turned him into something that not even I expected. Rather than use the blessing to perform great things and install the change he so desperately wanted, he conformed to the primordial urges and set himself on the warpath. The blessing changes you. It can change you for the better, but it can just as easily allow you to get lost in it."

Esta looked to Sana, her shoulders raised. Staring at the maiden of the sky, the illustrious moon. There was no pain or forlorn that swam in her pools of scarlet. It was fear. Deep within her eyes, Esta saw fear in the princess of the Sanguinaire.

Esta wiped some of the dried blood on her lip and turned to face away from the campfire, and said, "Did you kill him?"

Sana breathed slowly out of her nose and said, "Silthar forbids us from slaying fellow Sanguinaire. I had no choice but to leave him to his ways."

Esta shook her head, "But we killed a Visceran; he was a vampire. I could feel it."

Sana responded, "They are different. These Skithik that call themselves vampires are a disease. When they fed on the blood of their God for power, it did not change their spirit. It changed their bodies. They are more animal than they are mortal."

"Then… what did you do with him?"

Leaning back, Sana propped her hands behind her, "I walled him off in his manor. I locked him in the bowels. I feared what he would do should he be allowed to be released. I replaced him with someone that looked like him to ensure that nothing changed for the people he governed."

Her eyes had a despondent look as she finished, "I can still hear him in my mind. I can hear his cries for escape. And his screams of vengeance."

Esta shook her head and said, "Gods above…."

She stared down at her right hand. The memories of the muted screams played out in her mind. The woman looked like Esta.

Sana rested her hand on Esta's shoulder and said, "It's not easy what you're about to face. You'll see and hear people in your mind; that's the dark soul within trying to corrupt you."

Rubbing her index and middle finger against her thumb, the dried blood flaked onto the ground as she said, "How do you stop it?"

Sana leaned in close and said, "You don't. It never goes away, but you can keep the voices quiet and push the people you see in your mind to distant corners. It's not something you can slay; it's something you have to tame."

Esta rested her hand on Sana's and said, "Thank you…I needed that."

The half-elf looked to Sana as she stood up. Where once Esta would see someone that bore the undeserved mantle of deity, she saw someone grounded. Like the sorrow that ran through her, Esta saw countless more behind her crimson eyes. A wounded soul just like Esta's.

She stared into the fire and grappled with the reality of being one of the Hands of Silthar. If she was worthy. Doubt began to flood her mind as she stared into the bright flame, the moon reaching its apex and bringing with it a chilling wind. The weight of a rebellion eased out of her as she found herself getting lost in the lapping flames.

***

The fire died, and morning came. Esta took her time to reconfigure her armour. The golden armour they collected had tarnished entirely, whether by some latent magic or the damp air Esta could not figure out. Regardless, at the very least, she now had a full suit of armour, rolling her shoulder to test the weight of the spaulder.

Her other shoulder was bare, leaving her ancestral mark for all to see. She rested her hand on it and recalled the taste of blood she had fed from the woman the night before.

She clenched her free hand and said, "May it be the last innocent blood I spill."

Esta led them into the moors, with Sana on her left and Vedus on the right. They were a step or two behind her.

Sana asked as they walked along the makeshift trail that had been eroded by time, "Do we know to whom this village belonged?"

Esta thought for a moment and said, "Humans, I believe. But I'm not entirely sure. The huts might be too big for humans. If you could even call them huts anymore."

Vedus piped up, "There are theories that we descended from giants, that Uthos chose a few tribes of giants to be his chosen children and made them considerably smaller."

It did not take them long to reach the time-worn village. Their footsteps were loud on the long-dead weeds, and grass sprouted without abandon. The swamp overproduced water for the nearby vegetation; most of the grass and weeds had died ages ago without the Sylvanaire to care for them.

Esta rested her hand on the hilt of her sword; there was something about the village that she did not like. Caution was a soldier's ally, and her aunt often told her when she was still presiding in Rath.

Sana split off and ran her fingers over the mossy walls of one of the ruined buildings. "How strange…"

As Vedus and Esta stopped, Esta looked back and asked, "What is it?"

"This moss," Sana continued as she ran her fingers up and down the damp green sponge, "This is Veil Lichen. It's only supposed to grow deep underground."

Vedus rested his hand on his sword and asked, "What would cause it to grow above ground?"

Esta carefully drew her fingers from the moss as if she did not want to disturb whatever it was. She brushed her fingers against it and said in a muted tone, "I'm not sure… let's see what else we can find."

They continued, moving closer to the village centre. The village itself was perhaps three hundred metres from end to end. It was a considerable size, quite large in terms of an ancient tribe. Esta's knowledge of ancient human civilisation was very limited. The most she could recall was the numerous tribes of humankind dotted around the world of Calisine. The elves would often unearth ancient tools and bodies of the humans' long-forgotten past. The only other detail she could recall was when their first king united the tribes, Nar'Zhan Ghuul.

The centre of the village encircled them all around, the land was tightly packed, and the walkways were considerably less damp.

Sana pushed ahead slightly as she said, "The centre of the village serves as the epicentre of culture within a given tribe. If we are to find any answers as to what tribe this was and what else we can find, it would be here. But we should make this quick; we shouldn't stay here long."

***

After close to an hour and a half, they returned to the centre with what they found. Esta found various oddly shaped objects. She did not recognise them as utensils that ancient humans would use. One was a key of some kind; the other was bindings. Yet what was odd was the carapace-like exterior that mimicked the shell of an insect that the shackles took shape of.

Vedus found carcasses, not of humanoids but of a strange grub with many teeth. It was hardened and petrified, looking as though it screamed with its last breath. Even Esta did not recognise the species of the worm. She had never known a grub to have such terrifying teeth.

After some deciphering, Sana found various maps and documents that mentioned the name of a city. After knowing the city's name Vedus and Esta watched as Sana pulled back with a look of fear in her eyes. The city's name was Alrizhod.

Esta asked, "What's wrong?"

Sana choked back and replied, "Alrizhod is an ancient city that belonged to the Ilthauns."

Vedus seemed disturbed by this revelation and protested, "But all of the cities that belonged to them were uprooted and destroyed centuries ago."

Sana tossed the maps and documents carved into the animal's skins and shook her head as she said, "But look at how ancient this place is. We are the first mortals to walk upon this ground in— the Patheon knows how long. I'm not willing to take that chance. We are not going to that city."

Esta protested and reached out to Sana's mind and said, *"If we are supposed to mount a rebellion against the Skithik, we'll likely find what we need there."*

"No."

Vedus looked at both of them with confusion and said, "What?"

Esta replied before Sana could speak, "Nothing, we—"

Sana pressed her palm against Vedus's head and performed the same spell she cast on her. Only this time, her eyes grew wide in horror, and she clutched the sides of her head and screamed.

Vedus raised an eyebrow in confusion and said as he tried to help her to her feet, "What happened?!"

Esta helped Sana to her feet and said, "She tried to connect psychically with you, but something happened."

Sana shook her head, *"My suspicions were correct. The Shadow Queen has resurrected and left part of her magic in him. I fear she has chosen him for something terrible."*

Esta nodded, *"Great. Another God's influence that we have to worry about. But Sana, think about it. We have been scrounging for the last day or so on the run from the Skithik. We still need to mount a rebellion against the Skithik; we can't do that if we can barely protect ourselves with the scraps that we have found so far. But if we go to Alrizhod and search for supplies and perhaps a place to rest, then I see no harm in that. I'd wager the Skithik would prefer to leave that place alone."*

Sana shook her head, an ancient fear clouding her eyes as she said, *"No, there is nothing that we will find there other than madness."*

Esta's expression darkened, saying, *"We have no other options, and we are running out of time."*

Uncomfortable with this plan, she sighed and said, *"Fine...but we must stay together while we search for anything that we can use against them. And I don't want to hear complaints if one of us goes insane."*

Esta snatched the papers out of Sana's hands and said, "Then we go insane together."

Vedus raised his hand and said, "I'm very sorry, but what in Nosgora are you talking about?"

Sana replied, "If we are going to escape, we need to get the Skithik off us. To do that, we need better supplies. Esta feels as though we should go to Alrizhod and find it. But being that it is a former city belonging to mind devourers, I feel it is a bad idea."

Esta looked up from the map she was deciphering, Vedus nodded, "As crazy as this sounds, I agree with her. There's a reason the Skithik have not touched the grounds of Alrizhod in centuries. Despite the obvious dangers that might be inside, it's our best option."

Sana and Esta looked at one another as they heard the shuffling of brush and moss from their acute supernatural hearing far off in the distance, the Skithik drew closer.

Sana said, "The Skithik are close. We have to leave. Now!"

They rushed through the dense brush of the swamp and haphazardly guided themselves through the swamp's murky waters. Esta looked at the hideous runes carved into the animal skins. The lines were jagged and appeared as if carved with hate. She could not help but wonder if the fear that Sana felt was founded in reality. The Ilthauns were an ancient foe of the mortals from the first eras of recorded history. Sana's ancestors served as slaves to them for almost a century.

Esta could not help but understand her fear, but they had no other choice. They must uncover what secrets they could find in Alrizhod. For better or for worse.

Chapter Ten: Rage of Blood

Sana

Charging through the thickets of the swamp, they rushed to flee the awaiting blades of the Skithik. They trudged through thick patches of soft soil, bleeding with the murky deluge surrounding them. Sana knew not how many had found them, but if they were willing to send one of the Skavarn from their previous encounter, another awaited them or something much worse.

Esta charged ahead of them, Vedus and Sana on her heels as she read from the maps, charging through the swamp to decipher the ancient texts. She could see her tense her shoulders in frustration and divert her path to the side.

Sana asked, catching her breath, "What's the matter?"

Esta fumbled through the maps and said, "I can't decipher them while running. I need you two to keep the Skithik busy while I go through these texts."

Sana cursed, "You couldn't decipher it beforehand?"

Esta stepped to Sana threateningly and said, "What happened to *we have to leave now*?"

Vedus stepped between them and said, "Stay here and decipher it. We'll give you as much time as possible."

Sana shook her head and followed Vedus as they stepped out from their clearing and into the thickets. They brought themselves low to the ground. Sana's patchwork leather coat floated on the water's surface as she crouched.

Waving her hand through the air, she closed her eyes as she cast a spell. Opening her eyes, she saw the hilt of a blade in the shadows that they knelt in. She grabbed the hilt and pulled forth a longsword writhing and made of solidified shadows.

Testing the weight, she readied for an ambush. She listened to the wind, discerning their location from their hissing and growling. They drew close, and as they came closer, she motioned for Vedus to pay attention to her.

Vedus looked over, and Sana mimed, "On my mark: 3...2...1!"

They burst from the brush, her shadow sword roiling with sinister black wisps. Her cold shadow steel found flesh. It pierced a Skithik's throat cleanly, and the shaved flesh fell into the awaiting swamp water.

Without pause, she parried the strike of another Skithik that took the place of their fallen ally. She stepped into a proper fighting stance and remembered her training in the art of blade dancing. Taught by her father, she unleashed a series of quick strokes. The series of strikes were quick thrusts followed by a wide overhead strike, Viper's Caress, it was called.

The Skithik stepped forward after backpedalling from Viper's Caress in a horizontal strike at a seemingly exposed part of her stance. This was the strategy of blade dancing, to feign exposure to allow the fluidity of sword and spell.

She summoned bright red energy that solidified and collided with the Skithik's axe. The energy wrapped around the hatchet, and she telekinetically guided it away from her, exposing his left side.

Thrusting her finishing blow, known as the heart strike, her shadow blade pierced cleanly through skin and flesh. Blood flowed down the length of her blade. Her eyes flashed with bright red energy, roiling red mist rose through the air as she entered a state of what many Sanguinaire referred to as blood rage.

She felt herself bond with her blade, a specialised technique taught by her father in the Sanguinaire form of blade dancing, Lamenter's Waltz. A blood-crazed state, which powered the strikes and energy with each kill from her blade. She drank deep the mortal essence that leached into her blade and seeped into her. She was wreathed in bright red energy, a conduit of pure necrotic energy. However, she remembered the warning about using

Lamenter's Waltz. As your power grows in the stance, the more vulnerable you are to magical attacks.

She stepped, bursting through the air towards a group of Skithik, weapons raised and a glint of sadistic glee in their eyes.

It was a blur, even though she could not keep up with the swift strokes. From an onlooker's perspective, it would appear as though she was dancing; to some, it was a sinister waltz of blood and death. What was certain was the quick and clean death of the first Skithik.

She paused for a moment, her wreath of crimson energy expanding, bursting with life as the coordinated strikes of the Skithik ceased in the air. Summoning, in her palm, a sphere of swirling red and black energy, the wind kicked up as she pumped her hand into the air.

As she pulled her hand down, she willed their spirits to absorb into the sphere. Crimson mortal essence, from either side of her, drained from the Skithik, causing their forms to wither and die.

She clutched the now pulsating sphere and crushed the orb of energy. Her veins alight with pure energy. Sana felt her muscles boil with activity, and her mind filled in a drunken stupor of ecstasy. Her magical reserves filled. She could not help but have a sadistic smile on her face. With each death, she felt her magical reserves grow to heights she had not felt before. She finally had an outlet for her boiling hatred for the Skithik that enslaved her.

Her coat and hair bellowed in the air that kicked up, and waves of Skithik waited for them at their heels.

Vedus looked over at Sana in their pause and flourished his blade as they both waited for further violence.

The prince said, "You seem to be enjoying yourself."

Sana smiled and raised her voice over the swirling storm of mortal essence, "You have no idea how long I have waited for this moment."

As she readied her stance, she heard Esta in her mind. *"All right, I'm ready."*

Sana growled briefly, her drunken state of power now dissipating slightly as she replied, *"On our way."*

Lamenter's Waltz was a hard state to exit from. It was easy to lose oneself and have one's mind slowly devolve into a state of pure primal desire to satiate the dark spirit within, that raging spirit of murderous glee; the Sangilis it was called. The cruel dark reflection of a soul that inhabited all vampires, Sanguinaire and otherwise. Every vampire was threatened to enter this state. Once one succumbed to it, all sense of self would be lost, becoming the monster society believes them to be. The older and more powerful one becomes, the more susceptible they are to devolving into this state.

She calmed her Sangilis, letting go of her shadow sword, and willed it out of existence in a puff of shadows. She willed the swirling energy around her into her weaving hands. She spoke in the Sanguinaire dialect of Zarlonian, the language of magic. It was a series of words that promised action against her enemies.

The energy pulsated with each pass of her hands, the energy threatening to burst out and lap the mortal essence she possessed. Finishing the spell, she burst her hands out in a cone, and the energy spread out and connected with many of the Skithik. Crimson energy wrapped around them, slowing their muscles.

Vedus lowered his sword for a moment as Sana caught her breath, her mind dizzy from the state she left and said, pressing two fingers to her temple. "Come, she has finished deciphering the maps."

Vedus reached out for a moment and asked while sheathing his blade, "Will you be all right?"

"Yes, I'll be fine," Sana said earnestly. "Dizzy, that's all."

They rushed back and followed the brush to where they had left Esta to decipher the maps. She could feel the blood-crazed beast that slumbered once more that always threatened to take over her mind if she let it. It had been quite some time since she interacted with it, not since starting her bloodline. At that moment, she realised Esta had not yet faced that part of vampirism. She was still just a fledgling. Seeing so much spilt blood will do that. It can awaken that ancient spirit that resides within all vampires. And it was something that Esta would have to face alone. Sana worried that she might succumb to it.

She buried the thought as they met with Esta, who raised the maps and said, "This way!"

***

Bursting from a belt of trees, they once more stumbled onto the tightly packed ground. Only this time, as they stepped onto the ground, it felt different.

Sana felt a surge of energy move through her, an ancient feeling coursing through her veins. They did not belong, treading upon such ancient and cursed soil.

She looked up and saw the time-worn buildings, large obsidian shadows created by the stars above. The material of the buildings was such that they mirrored the night sky. If one did not know where the city was, it could be easily missed. They rose high and matched the height of the trees.

It filled her with equal amounts of awe and fear. They still did not know what sinister trappings awaited them within its walls.

Sana looked to Esta, who was more awestricken than fear-stricken, and said, "Alrizhod."

Their gawking ceased as they heard a roar that awoke the night itself. There was no time to turn as they saw a blur of hulking scaly muscle burst into their midst, erupting the air around them with powerful magical energy, causing all of them to lift from the ground.

Sana righted herself, familiar with such forces of arcana. Reaching out her hands and summoning winds to lower herself slowly and carefully to the ground. Vedus and Esta did not have such luck.

Vedus collided with the obsidian stone building a few metres away, collapsing to the ground. Esta had similar luck, but she skidded against the ground, grunting against the pain of each strike of earth. Sana summoned her shadow sword and looked at the figure that caused harm to her and her companions.

He stood the same as the previous Skavarn that attacked them before, but this one was different. Wrapped around one arm was a shroud that bore the insignia of the noble house of the Skavarn. It was a web of hatches and scratchings against a field of crimson. His armour bore the colour of rust. Scars flowed around his snout, having a more weathered and seasoned look about him. Then she saw the blade at his side and remembered the tales of the Skithik that spoke this one's name. This was Telarth the Headhunter. Though filled with dread, she readied her blade and waited for her opponent to strike, the blood rage seething throughout her and yearning to taste his mortal essence.

Chapter Eleven: The Apex Predator

Esta

Esta's ears rang with the toll of pain and death. Beaten and battered, she struggled to push herself up off the ground. Her muscles attempted to lift her.

Raising her head, she saw the large headhunter and Sana begin battling. Her shadow blade was quick, but Telarth did not let up and parried and blocked each strike. There was an unbound fury that stung in her eyes, pumped through her veins, and seeped into her strikes. Controlling the anger unleashed with every strike, Esta saw this look when she returned from distracting the Skithik.

Finding a pause in her assault, he manoeuvred to her side and raised his hook blade. Sana raised her off-hand and summoned a barrier of red energy as the hook blade came down.

Esta bit back the pain and forced herself to her feet, leaning against her hands while on her knees. With each step, she felt a tightening around her head and clenched her jaw at the ever-increasing pain. Some of her ribs were likely broken, and she might be fighting a concussion very well, but she needed to help Sana since Vedus was still recovering from the thunder wave.

She pulled her shield from her back and unsheathed her sword as she shakily stood back up. Flourishing her blade, she sized up the Head-Hunter.

He saw Esta stand up. A sadistic smile crossed his reptilian lips as he said, "Such arrogance. Thinking that you can evade the will of the Skithik. You are no longer free; your will belongs to the Skithik."

Telarth paused his assault, causing Sana to reform the crimson energy and form a solidified wave of energy that threatened to severe Telarth's torso from shoulder to hip.

Raising his off-hand, he grabbed the energy firmly, and the air rippled and warped with the collapsing arcane energy. They struggled there for a moment.

"May my sword swing true and my shield holdfast."

Using the time, Esta raised her shield and charged forward. Fervour pumped her veins and numbed the pain that engulfed her sides and head.

Hooking the shadow blade, he knocked Sana off balance, still gripping the energy. He reformed the arcane energy, and the energy vortexed and churned with power in his clawed palm. It crackled and hissed as he burst his hand out. Tongues of scarlet lightning leapt from his open palm.

Sana weaved scarlet arcane in her hands. *"Keep him distracted."*

"Hard not to!"

It collided with her shield; the force pushed her back and tested her strength. She powered through the continuous streams of arcane electricity. With each step, she could feel her pained form trudge forward.

The force ceased, and she finished her charge, pulling her shield back that still crackled with energy, and went to bash the headhunter.

He sidestepped to avoid the coming force of the shield and parried her sword slash. He slammed his palm against the top of the shield and gripped it hard. Before she could contest his strength, he already lifted her off the ground and swung her.

She collided with Sana as she pushed herself back up, and they tumbled back.

Her head and sides flared with pain; she bit back a cry of agony. She closed her eyes, pushing against the suppressive force of the rising tide of pain that threatened to overtake her. For a moment, she felt her eyes cloud as she almost got pulled into unconsciousness. But she fought back, biting against the anguish, and pushed herself back to her knees.

Sana helped her to her feet, grim determination in her eyes. Esta nodded and shook her hand, and prepared herself.

Telarth smirked again, grabbing what looked to be a net from his leather belt, and said, "I expected more from the Hands of Silthar."

Sana furrowed her brow. "How did—"

"The stench of his godly presence has left its mark on you." Telarth's scarred face beamed with elation at the thought of continuing their fight, "Poor wretches. Silthar's era of ruling over blood is over. Soon we will take his throne, and all vampires will submit to our will or be destroyed."

Brandishing his hook blade, he continued, "I'd offer you to surrender, but I'd rather hear you beg for it."

Esta bashed her sword against her shield defiantly as she readied herself. Her sides flared, and her mind clouded; Esta briefly moved her eyes to Vedus, who now collected himself and saw the fight. Peeling back into the shadows, he disappeared.

They charged, and Sana leapt as Esta charged forward. Their swords poised to strike, he sidestepped, parried Sana's downward slash, and swung his hook blade down towards Esta. It collided with her shield.

Unleashing his net, it wrapped around Sana as she limply fell back to the ground. Her head slammed against the stone floor. Reinvigorated, Esta unleashed strikes against the headhunter. He easily blocked each strike, his smile ever-increasing as her anger boiled over.

She could feel her rage polluting her veins and numbing the pain in her sides and head. Over the sound of clashing steel, she heard him mock her, "Yes, succumb to it. Let it overtake your mind."

She could feel a force envelope her mind, overtaking her thoughts and actions—something deep within, something that she beat back every day since she acquired vampirism. In the raging tempest in her mind, she heard Sana as she painfully shouted, "No, you're not ready. Esta. Don't let it overtake you!"

Her vision filled with red as her clouded mind ceased, blissfully clear. She felt a euphoric rush run across her veins and muscles. Renewed fervour pumped through her as she unleashed a faster and stronger assault than before. The air rippled around her, warping with a vortex of energy.

Her vision cleared as she watched Telarth struggle to block and parry her unrelenting attacks. Pushing him towards the edge of the obelisk-like structure they stood upon.

The distorted air pulsated with energy as she pushed him to the very edge of the platform.

She breathed heavily as the strain of this state she entered began to take its toll.

In a downward slash, he guided her sword away, exposing herself. She heard Sana release herself from her net and shout, "NO!"

Esta watched helplessly as Telarth's hook blade came down and sliced cleanly through her arm at the elbow. The euphoria, distorted air, and rage-induced state she entered all paused as she screamed in pain. She howled, shaking the air with a scream that defied the quiet. She shook and shivered with the sudden lack of her left arm.

She collapsed to her knees, clenching her eyes shut as she fought back the tears. Her stump flared, stinging with white-hot pain. She quivered, her mind still swimming. The rage-induced state caused her to keep consciousness, but she wanted to let her mind take her far away from the unbearable pain.

Esta looked up; the looming headhunter imposed a great deal of fear. She saw him take the form of a spectre of death for a brief moment, ready to sever her soul from this plane to Silthar's blasphemous realm of blood and undeath.

He raised his hook blade, ready to decapitate Esta, yet Sana charged forward and leapt through the air towards Telarth, their swords collided over Esta's head.

Her eyes opened, and fear and despair overtook her as she saw her severed arm lying limply near the platform's edge, on top of her shield.

It was all too much, she desperately wanted to fall unconscious and forfeit for a brief moment that she lost her arm. That the Skithik was hunting her. That she was one of the Hands of Silthar. That she was even a vampire.

They struggled against one another. Esta heard Telarth after he briefly chuckled, "You're next."

Then she saw one of the shadows move, leaping from what seemed from thin air, Vedus materialised, and while Telarth had his attention elsewhere, he reversed his glimmering gold blade.

It found its way into the Skavarn's hulking back, piercing deep through a gap in his armour. The blade poked through his chest, showering Esta with fresh blood.

"How... in the name of Uthos... did he puncture... through a breastplate... with a weakened sword?" The blood coated her face; by reflex alone, she licked her lips, tasting his cold blood. The swirling vortex of pain subsided

briefly as she felt the state solidify itself in her mind. She did it and failed what she fought for months to beat back. She succumbed fully to her vampirism.

Telarth gasped; with no words left to exchange, Sana pulled her sword back, and with a primal screech, she severed Telarth's head from his shoulders. The blade did not go cleanly through the first time, showering Esta once more in blood. The second time, however, the head rolled off and away.

Esta was now drenched as the body of Telarth collapsed to the ground, all life leaving the Skithik headhunter. Drenched in blood and relieved, she exhaled before looking up into the treeline. There were creeping shadows. They were fear-stricken, whispering amongst themselves. All of them stepped slowly back until no forms remained. They were the rest of the Skithik, and they witnessed one of their most prized warriors fall to two rebel vampires and a shadow-cursed prince.

She smiled briefly before collapsing into unconsciousness. Though she hated herself even more now, at least there was hope that remained. Her heart fluttered at the thought they had moments to rest. She closed her eyes as Vedus and Sana rushed to help her, accepting the numbing darkness.

Chapter Twelve: The City Of Nightmares

Sana's mind drowned in endless possibilities. She drowned in sorrow, in pain. The wretched thing had severed Esta's arm. She felt useless, unable to protect her and keep her safe. Sana drowned in her own self-loathing; doubt had been cast upon her. She questioned everything now. Was she capable of leadership? How could she have let this happen? She stood there, watched it happen, and did nothing.

As her mind raced, she shuffled the unconscious form of her bonded friend, Esta. They had been through so much that a fraction of tension still existed between them. Yet that did not stop her from caring for her.

She looked back and saw Vedus holding her shield and her severed arm. The sight alone made her stomach turn.

They brought her into a small building with only one room and used the same black stone that all other buildings used. As they crossed the threshold, Sana could feel a considerable temperature difference despite having no door. She took note of that fact and stored it away for later; now, she had a dying companion to take care of.

Pulling off her cloak, she laid it on the floor, Vedus doing the same, resting her arm and shield off to the side and laying his cloak over Sana's. She lowered the half-elf unto the cloaks and knelt next to her, closing her eyes and easing her swimming mind. The blood flow was not as intense as it had been a few minutes ago. It gently oozed onto the blanket. Like any vampire, her blood was darker, almost black. The ichorous mortal essence seeped onto their lizard skin cloaks. Specks of blood dotted her now long white hair and her youthful face.

Sana reached out and asked, "Hand me her arm."

Vedus handed over the arm, nervousness overtaking him. She tried to exude confidence to ease his mind.

As she calmed her mind, she began the procedure she remembered from what the blood priests had taught her about regrafting a limb to the body.

Sana procured a small dagger and asked, "I need you to hold her down as well."

Vedus lifted an eyebrow, "But she's unconscious?"

She nodded, "Yeah, that doesn't mean that she stops feeling pain because of that. Now hold her down, and no matter how painfully she screams, do not let go."

The prince nodded and got into position for the procedure to begin.

Sana took the knife and set it aside. Inspecting both arm and stump carefully, she removed the damaged tissue. As all of the Skithik's weapons were at least tempered with silver, the wounds were slightly cauterised, which helped stop the blood flow but not with reattaching her limb.

Slowly she shaved off the thin layer of damaged flesh and sinew, and a few gasps of pain erupted from Esta's unconscious form. Her heart sank. Doubt and hope battled within her mind with only grim determination to guide her.

She worked quickly, as the flesh had already begun to heal. She raced to keep up with the regrowing tissue. Frustration and anger rose within her, still hanging on the face that she could have done something to stop this.

Biting her lips, she brought the knife to the exposed bones of her stump and slowly but surely carved and shaved her bone. Esta howled in pain. Nothing wounded Sana's heart more than hearing her woeful cries.

Once the bones were sufficiently shaved, she brought the severed limb over to Esta and broke off pieces of her chainmail shirt underneath her armour.

She quickly fashioned them into wires and attached them to the bones. A scream rose once more. Esta's nightmarish cries would haunt Sana for the rest of her days.

Using her magic, she slowly cast a spell, summoning the will of her blood, her tissue, and her muscle to cooperate. Focusing, she slowly repaired the damaged arm. Sweat dripped from the top of her brow as she concentrated on keeping her content and restoring what had been lost.

***

It had taken her two hours before it was done, and the wounds were dressed correctly. Sana's mind settled back from frustration but still wracking the prayers of the followers of Silthar. For days she heard their whispers, their prayers to the father of blood and lineage. To anyone else, they might have been driven mad. Sana held herself together; she had to. She was to lead her people against the Skithik. Even if doubt settled in her mind, she needed to put aside her feelings and push through. It never left, though. Self-doubt crept in around her at all hours.

Vedus returned. When Sana was healing Esta's wounds, she asked him to find himself food. He returned with three rabbits.

She sat on the step of the small building, taking in the maddening view of the city. Her jaw clenched as she heard her bloodline whisper to her. They struggled. They needed her once more, and their faith in her was breaking. Sana understood; perhaps she was not strong enough. Helplessly, she watched as Telarth severed Esta's arm; all she could do was watch. Centuries-old, she was caught helplessly by a net.

Before madness began to settle into her mind, Vedus handed her a rabbit. She grabbed it and said, "Thank you."

Vedus set his other quarry down and nodded to the building behind her, "How is she?"

Moving the rabbit from her awaiting teeth for a moment, "She'll survive. It might take some time for her to recover fully. What took so long was her body trying to self-repair the wound and heal over it. Her muscles will have to get used to renewed mobility. But yes, she will be fine."

Vedus sat next to her and said, "If I recall correctly, you seemed worried for her survival."

Sana drank a mouthful of blood before she stopped and replied, "Of course I did; she is the other Hand of Silthar; I have every right to worry about her well-being."

Vedus gestured with his knife and said, "Yes, but you seem to have bonded with her already. No hint of the rivalry I felt between you two when you rescued me."

Sana let her eyes drift down, taking in his words. There was some truth to them. She had started to bond with her. She felt like a protective older sister to Esta. Though she doubted Esta felt the same way. She had watched her grow with vampirism from months upon months of staying in her fledgling state. Esta was heroborn. It was hard for Sana not to be inspired to do better. Sana grappled with those feelings and used them to reinforce her resolve. For Esta and her bloodline.

After taking another drink from the rabbit, she mused, nearly depleting the tiny creature into dried meat. "How could I not? Our rivalry was childish; for us to carry on together, we either needed to grow beyond this petty rivalry or let it consume us and forsake our duty to Silthar. We both, I believe, have no intentions of forsaking the will of Silthar, so I hope she has had the same thoughts as I."

"Can't you read her thoughts because of that telepathic bond?"

Taking the last drop of blood from the rabbit, she tossed it aside. Satisfied with her meal, she leaned against the stone stairs, "I would not dare forsake her trust and do such a thing. She has left her fledgling state, the first stage of vampirism. It is not a curse but more of a personification of every mortal race's primal thoughts and feelings, just amplified. Silthar's blessing allows a small window, not for the carrier, but for the vampirism itself to decide if the carrier is worthy of Silthar's blessing."

Vedus finished dressing his rabbit and began to clean the small hide, pausing for a moment as he said, "Has Esta been proven worthy?"

Sana shrugged, "I do not know for sure. Typically, at least in the case of the Sanguinaire, the next eldest vampire of your bloodline is to guide you and prepare you for the next stage in accepting the gifts of vampirism."

"Why did you not prepare Esta?"

Sana gulped; she had not considered that level of guilt, "If she is found unworthy of the gifts of Silthar, then I have failed not just myself but my bloodline. Pushing a fledgling to the next stage of vampirism when they are not prepared are rendered as Feral, a fate worse than death."

Vedus tightened his lips for a moment and said, "My apologies for worrying you."

Sana raised her hand and said, pleading, "It's all right. She is one of the Desidarius; she will pull through. She has to."

Vedus nodded, gathering the properly dressed rabbit and fur, and said, "I am going to start a fire to cook my meal. If you need me, I will not be far away."

Sana nodded and watched him walk away to the other side of the building. She could see the look in his eyes. He was struggling to maintain his sanity against the maddening shadows. Bargaining for power with Satris always had its drawbacks. The one that stood out most often seemed to be hearing the voices of shadows wherever one goes. She did not envy him, but she understood him personally. Even at that moment, she could still hear the prayers of Silthar's children.

"Hand... of... Sil... thar..." Sana burst to her feet, looking for the source of that voice, thinking that she had heard it aloud for a moment. Flicking her hands, she summoned reserved spells, her hands dancing in red energy.

As she thought about it, she realised it was a psychic voice. Calming her body, she replied to it, *"Who are you? And what do you want?"*

There was no reply, and she wandered away from the building, out of the eyes of her companions, in case it was some enemy. Testing the voice, she sent a wave of psychic energy, she was not familiar with psychic magic, but she had known the basics taught by the Blood Priests.

She felt something in her mind shift, something bid her to walk, and it was not of her own volition. Sana could not resist and walked off with fear rising in her veins.

"I... am... no... enemy..."

"How can I know for sure?" Sana replied.

"Already… dead… you… would be…" It strained, not to maintain the psychic connection, but to keep itself alive. Whatever being this was. She wandered through the streets, feeling an ancient familiarity with its streets. She stepped not against her will, but more of following a familiar trail long once thought forgotten did not help her fear of the city.

Sana passed the city centre, leaving the northeast corner where they resided. It was wide and could have thousands of people comfortably standing there. The Ilthauns had the Elves and Dwarves kept as slaves. It only seemed appropriate.

She had passed the onyx-coloured ziggurat in the centre, the city's tallest and most imposing building. It climbed eighty-two metres high, widening at the base and slowly becoming smaller as it reached the peak. A small opening was wide enough for two people at the top.

She moved down a tight alley, the cursed geometry threatening to drive her insane. The walls appeared to move closer to her, threatening to squash her. She continued, certain of her demise. Closing her eyes, she waited for one of the spectres of death to ferry her away.

When none came, she opened her eyes. A small room opened around her, darkness cloaking the location and size of her room. A darkness that not even she could see through. Her mind was being tricked. She knew it. One powerful enough in the realm of psychic magic could alter the reality of those around, driving them insane or succumbing to their superior wills. She felt no such imposing force, only that she needed to be there.

She stopped in what she could only assume was the centre. The darkness moved away from her as the voice became clearer, *"You are proficient in... the magic of will..."*

"My people taught me much."

"What is a leader... without the grace and generosity of their... citizens."

"Why am I here?"

"With all of your gifts... you still... struggle with the voices of the present."

"Why is this important to you? Whomever you might be?"

"Not... whoever..."

It paused, and suddenly the reality in front of her warped and changed. A small pedestal rose in front of her. Upon it was a crown. Spikes rose from the tightly tempered iron, cresting the head in front. It was jagged and wrapped snugly around the head in uncomfortable iron rods. At the top of it, fitting just above the middle of the forehead, was an eye. It was milky and blinked long.

The voice continued, *"Whatever... I am an artefact... given life by the previous inhabitants... once I was a loyal servant... one of the chosen slaves to become part of their cult... not as a sacrifice... but I was to prove my worth to their... hideous God... when the slaves rose, I put my conscious into this crown... for centuries I have been within my mind waiting for someone worthy to come upon... the black city... and... here you are... Sana Nailo..."*

She raised an eyebrow, *"So I am to trust the words of a sentient crown that once was a servant of the Ilthauns? Who gave themselves from their chaos masters to the Void Pantheon?"*

"If my intentions were—"

"To harm then you would have done so. Yes, you said that before. But if I don you, how am I supposed to believe that you won't overtake my mind."

"A wise precaution... I cannot... as powerful as my psychic abilities might be... my consciousness is too damaged... I could perhaps take over your mind for an hour or so before... you and I both would deteriorate... this is not my wish."

Sana said nothing, reaching out to the crown, sifting through its large breadth of memories. She could sense no ill intentions.

It spoke again, *"Don me… and I can help you… I can teach you how to improve your… psychic will… reach out to your bloodline…"*

She hesitated. She could not rationalise just taking the crown from a long-lost Ilthaun city without something in return. She suspected that there was something that the crown was not telling her. Despite the sound logic, she could not do it.

She grabbed the crown and replied, *"I will take you with me. Prove to me you do not intend to overtake my mind, and I will don you. Prove otherwise, and I will destroy you. Do we understand each other?"*

She sensed frustration growing within the sentient crown, thinking about what it could do. When nothing came up, that could persuade her. *"As you wish…"*

She hooked the crown to her belt and asked, *"What do I call you?"*

It thought for a long time, likely trying to remember the name it had from ten thousand years ago or more. She knew not the age of the Ilthaun empire, knew enough of it to know that it was before the death of Beros.

It replied, *"Drass… that was my name…"*

Turning around, she walked through the nightmarish geometry once more. As she walked through it, she noted that it steadily began not to bother her as much. Sana was unsure if that was something to be proud of or feared.

Chapter Thirteen: Stalker of The Shadows

Vedus

The comfort of his fire felt distant. Vedus tried to forget it. He tried to bury the thoughts of his sudden resurrection. Still, they whispered, silently snickering to themselves. Damning, laughing, cursing, screaming. They drowned his hearing with noise that he wished would cease. He tried everything, but nothing worked. On and on, they would murmur, even when he would talk with someone. Quieting for a moment, they would continue their maddening conversations.

Vedus shook. His nerves were constantly shot. He looked about his surroundings perhaps thousands of times, constantly on edge. His mind was quaking with insanity. He struggled through his meal, eyes widened with soul-shaken fear. Something crept beyond his vision; there had to be. Madness did not cloud his mind; something stalked him just beyond his vision. There had to be. There was no other solution, no other sane conclusion.

He clutched his sword with his other hand, ready to strike the stalker in the shadows.

The prince devoured his meal as quick as he could, whispering to himself as he finished, "You will come no closer, spectre of shadows. You will stay far away from me."

Rocking back and forth, he whipped his head around to find the source of this anxiousness. The gnashing shadows laughed at him, watching the show unfold before them.

He stood up in furious anger, pointed his sword toward many shadows, and shouted, "You foul abominations! Curse you and your ilk! Leave me be; I command you!"

"Leave…" He swung his sword wildly, striking nothing but open air.

"Me…" Bringing himself to the brush of the moors that festered with activity.

"…Be!" He drove his sword down into one of the trees, bearing a large, sinister-looking shadow.

He shivered, his shoulders drooping, and his head hung low. Vedus shook as he wept into his other hand, still gripping his sword. The prince wept not for his desire to have the whispers stop. He wept because he finally had succumbed. With its sizeable rusty iron hooks, Madness took a titanic grip upon him. He was descending further into madness; his grip on reality was wavering. Faltering under the maddening whispers of shadows, he knew not their names.

He lost his grip upon the embedded sword into the petrified tree, falling to his knees in the moors. The murky waters accepted his downtrodden slumping form. Vedus wept, the shadows no longer laughing but calmly whispering amongst themselves rather than directly at him. He could nearly lose his attention from them. The only thing that mattered was his damaged psyche.

"You let them in…"

"They killed you…"

"You died…"

"Why are you alive?"

"You should be dead!"

"Crawl back to the grave…"

His weeping continued, gulping large amounts of air to try and keep breathing. He felt lost and confused. Was there nothing upon Calisine that could bring him solace? Solace from the living hell he persisted in every day?

"Poor little prince…" Vedus shot up his head, finding the source of the physically manifesting voice. Distantly, he saw a figure stalking amongst shadows. It sauntered closer to him, a few metres out.

He rushed for his sword, pulled it out, pointed it toward the figure in the shadows, and said sternly, "Who are you?"

She said no words, continuing to walk in from the writhing shadows. In the clear moonlight, he saw her fully now. She wore a black gown, her skin was as pale as the snow, and her hair ebon black. Long sharpened nails came out from her fingers, sharpened at the ends. Dotting around her wrists and fingers were various gold wraps and jewellery of the finest quality. She wore a golden choker, connecting like a web around her neck and chest. Her eyes were fierce, like a man's when angry. They bore the colour and intensity of two cerulean nebulas. He fixed his gaze upon them as if he was obligated not to look away. Her hair was curled and was the colour of falling ash.

He could not turn away. She was the most beautiful woman he had ever seen.

She was two metres away, a delightful smile on her face, warm and inviting, as she said, "I will forgive your ignorance just this once. I am not as infamous as my mother or some of my sisters."

She moved her gaze past him for a moment and said, "The woes of being the youngest sibling, eh?"

Vedus willed himself to say something, choking back confusion as he said, "Who are you?"

She blinked, fixing her gaze upon him, and said, "You can call me Vastra, youngest of the Daughters of Shadow."

The Daughters of Shadow seemed vaguely familiar to him, but he could not place it. He did know that she was some demigod or demigod-like being. His grip on his sword tightened.

She laughed at his unmoving stance. It had all the warmth of a crocodile's hiss.

She came closer, dancing two fingers on the blade's surface, and said, "Put your mortal weapon away. It will be of no use for you now."

He felt his muscles stiffen with attention as if his mind suggested following her commands. But he refused, keeping his muscles firm.

She gave a sinister smile, creeping in close, and said, "Quit putting on a brave face, Prince Vedus. I know what plagues you."

Vedus hesitated a moment and asked, "How?"

"I know the work of my mother when I see it. It was her magic that gave you life again."

He moved one of his hands to his throat, drawing his fingers across the scar left after the Night of Black Swords.

His mind swam with all manner of names until he realised who it was that gave him rise.

Vedus shook his head and said, "No… that's—that's impossible… she wields shadow magic, shadows cannot…."

She raised her finger to his lips, effectively silencing him as she said, "The shadows hold many secrets. But you already knew that, didn't you?"

The whispers rose in volume for a moment as if to answer her. A cruel smile crossed her lips as she said, "They can guide you if you let them. I can help you if you—"

He pushed against what psychic force had held him and drove his sword into Vastra's chest. She gasped, feeling the blade pierce into her ribcage.

With a fierce scowl, he tightened his jaw and said, "Do not attempt to take hold of my mind. I will not succumb to your whims. I will find a way to get rid of this, to silence the whispers, and then I will kill you."

She looked down at the blade, and with a smug look, she wrenched the blade deeper into her. She gripped his hand while gasping as she made her way down the blade. She threatened to crush his fingers with the force that grabbed hold of his mind.

He stared deep into her eyes; they swirled with intensity. Flaring and dancing with primal energy, she growled, "You already have, Vedus."

She leaned closer. The same psychic force instilled soul-crushing fear.

Whispering into his ear, she said in a husky tone, "I'm not even real...Vedus what are you doing?"

"Vedus?" Blinking, he gasped as he rubbed his eyes with one of his hands. There was no one in front of him. No sign of Vastra, only empty air. He heard the shuffling of feet in the murky waters. He jumped and turned around quickly with his sword raised. It was Sana. She had her hands raised, a confused look in her eyes.

He quickly sheathed his sword and coughed as he said, "Just... doing drills."

Sana furrowed her brow and said, "Alone? In the moors?"

He said nothing, a voice speaking loud in his head, *"There's an artefact, Vedus. It can dampen the whispers of darkness."*

Sana asked again, "Whom were you talking to?"

"I have installed a memory into you of the location of the armour. I am not your enemy."

Vedus breathed in, calming his swirling mind as he said, "No one… sorry, the city was starting to get to my head. Needed some space."

She nodded, her look not faltering as she said, "Okay… let me know next time that way, I know you didn't just wander off."

He nodded, looked at the crown on her belt, and said, "What's that?"

Her look faded, causing his mind to settle down, and she replied, "Something that might help us. Has Esta awoken yet?"

"No, not yet," he said, now sheathing his sword. "She's still resting from the last time I saw her."

She nodded and motioned for him to follow her back.

He recalled this memory that Vastra had given to her. It was nearby. If he were going to believe her and put his faith in the notion that she had no ill intentions, then he would have to find time for when Esta and Sana were sleeping. It was nearby, relatively close. He was inclined to believe her to some extent. Could she install fake memories? The succubi of Umral were deceitful, but they were never known to tell explicit lies. They bend the truth to fit their goals, whatever goal that might be… He knew it was a bad idea to get this armour, but he would be of no use to Esta and Sana if he lost his mind to insanity. Stepping back onto the black stone streets of Alrizhod, the fire died, and dawn peaked above the onyx spires of the city. The wind gave a sinister whistle as it wound its way through the twisted geometry of the obelisks of sleek shadows.

Sana stepped into the building and burst back out with a worried expression.

Vedus furrowed his brow and asked, "What's wrong? Is she okay?"

A mix of anger and fear rose within her as she said, "She's gone."

Chapter Fourteen: Sword of Memory's Lost

Esta

From the great darkness of unconsciousness, Esta gasped as she bid herself to rise once more. A haziness pervaded over her mind and eyes, raising her left arm as she tried to wipe the tiredness from her eyes. Yet she felt resistance.

It felt sore and bruised. She looked down at it, her eyes growing wide. She saw the wrapping red wound around her arm at the elbow. At that moment, she remembered the delimitation at Telarth's hand. The painful memory replayed in her mind.

Wiping her face, she frantically tried to clean her face of the dried blood. There was very little; most had been cleaned off. Flakes of dried blood scattered on the light breeze.

She looked around; she was in a small building in Alrizhod, two metres long by two metres wide. Esta awoke, laying on top of Skithik scale cloaks.

She stood up, noticing her chainmail had a few missing links. This struck her as odd, but she thought nothing of it. Her equipment was nearby. She grabbed her sword and shield as she left the building. She pulled her shield over her back and finished strapping her sword sheath to her belt.

As she did so, she asked loudly, "Sana? Vedus? Where are you?"

There was no answer, and she was too out of range to reach out with her telepathic connection to Sana. A camp had been set up, the embers of the campfire still clinging to life. Where could they have gone? She wandered beyond the bounds of their makeshift camp, looking for her wayward companions.

She felt different since she embraced vampirism, still disgusted at herself by that fact. Her hunger for blood remained, but it was not as intense as before. It felt less like a need and more like a lingering want. She felt stronger, more centred than before. Yet she could feel it, slumbering in the back of her psyche. The intense, primal emotions that vampirism amplified.

Esta walked through the empty streets of Alrizhod, the strange geometry confused her after some time, and she had to follow up to see if she had made any progress through the city. She sat in the company of the dying campfire and waited for her companions to find her again. The camp had not been broken. There was still a need to come back and grab their belongings.

She thought back to the fight with Telarth, their disjointed effort to kill the highly trained Skavarn warrior. Her muscles still ached, and were recovering from that fight. As she prodded and poked the dying embers with a stick, she thought back to all the training she had received over her many long years. Esta boiled with anger and self-hatred that she was unable to handle herself against Telarth. She was sure that if Ezran were there, he would have taken care of the headhunter handily. He was always better than her at wielding a blade. She thought back to their encounter during one of the battles of the Olkhan Invasion. They fought like half-elves. They were disciplined warriors and proved to be considerable foes against Rathain steel. They almost killed her, but her brother swooped in and saved her at the last moment.

She squeezed the stick tighter at that thought. So much doubt polluted her mind. Not just her envy of her brother but the disgrace she was upon the Desidarius name. She not only spilled the blood of many innocents, but she drank from them with unfettered revelry. On top of that, she allowed herself to be bested by an opponent. No wonder her afterlife was the realm of Silthar's. The rolling landscape of the blood plains filled her mind. Silthar's stoic face haunted her vision as she lingered upon that memory.

Her emotions were getting better, wiping her eyes of tears that had built up. She hated her life and all the cruelties she endured to survive and bring herself to that point.

She fell from her seat, collapsing to her hands and knees. Tears still ran down her cheeks as she prayed, "O' spirits of my ancestors, heed my call! I beg of you, give me guidance as to my future actions. I pray you guide me towards a better future."

Clenching the obsidian rock with her hands, she almost felt it break under her intense grips and whispered as she finished her prayer, "Please."

A deity never claimed half-elves. Therefore, they had no afterlife waiting for them. So, they decided to use magic to make their own. For generations, they perfected the art of trans-planar manipulation and landed upon the rituals of Reyarth. Or the Reyarthian Trials. These chosen Half-elves that take up the rituals of Reyarth are to become living conduits of planar energy and become walking demi-planes of existence. Each prominent family of the Half-elves has a Reyarthian Conduit. Once a conduit is nearing the end of its extended lifespan, it will choose a successor to take up its mantle.

Now that was robbed of her because of a curse granted by one of the cruellest Gods of the Pantheon. Her weeping quickly turned into quiet anger.

Then, she felt the air shift. She looked up and saw a few metres away a white wolf. It stood proud, its stoic expression never faltering as its eyes of stormy blue fixed themselves upon her. There was recognition in those eyes. This struck Esta as odd. The white wolf was the insignia of the Desidarius family, symbolising the destiny and power of the whole, not the individual.

It waited expectantly, never faltering in its gaze and promptly resting upon its haunches waiting for her. Esta stood up, wiping the tears away, and stalked closer to the white wolf. It did not flinch as she approached it.

She was a metre away, and it turned, motioning her to follow him. He was large, and runes etched unto him. Runes that belonged to an ancient arcane alphabet long before Zarlonian was created. What they said, however, she could not know for sure.

They stalked the barren moors. Not lost or wandering, Esta knew that she was being guided somewhere. Whether this was some lingering madness due to the unnatural geometry or the lingering affiliation from accepting vampirism, she did not know. That doubt willed her forward, despite her preconceived notions. Winding perhaps twenty yards away from the city, the white wolf stopped and sat again. Esta halted in her tracks and took in where the white wolf had taken her.

It was a mound that appeared to be covered with stones and rocks. At the crest of the mound was a sword embedded into the large mound.

Taking a closer look, the sword bore runes of the ancient language of Man. The runes of Dhrukk. Esta suspected that the Runes of Dhrukk had not been used since the days of Nar'Zhan Ghuul's unification. She could translate them. The half-elves used a very similar alphabet for their runic magic called Reythilian.

The name of the blade was Sephril. Esta heard tales that it was forged from a dying star, given to one of Nar'Zhan Ghuul's most decorated generals, Sephril the Heaven's Rage. Despite its age, it still bore the shimmer of polished silver as if from the days it was tempered in the forges of Gethlorian, Nar'Zhan Ghuul's capital. The surface of the blade reflected much. If one told Esta it was made from the pane of a mirror, she would have believed them. So pure and untouched, despite the thousands of orcs slain by Sephril when the civilization of Man drove them out from the shores of Ketos.

Esta shook her head, burying her memories of serving in the most recent Olkan Invasion effort led by Kodlan Khane. A grudge was still held between humans and orcs since that day. She prayed the civil war of the Human Empire did not shatter what unity remained for the orcs to take advantage of.

The hilt and some of the etchings were filled with a granite-like material with golden veins flowing around the surface. The Blood of Heaven, it was called, blessed by Uthos himself to serve its wielder well against any foe of the Pantheon.

Awestricken by Sephril, Esta motioned to pull it from the mound. She hesitated, worried unknown forces would strike her down for not being worthy to bear such an artefact. Her doubt gave her pause and told her not to dare grip such a timeworn relic.

A tear fell from her eye as she clenched her teeth and caressed her hand against the cold steel hilt. She did not want to succumb to her doubt and self-hatred anymore. She pulled the sword. The weight, despite being a bastard sword, was uncannily light. It was as if she held a feather in her hand. She could have sworn it chorused a bright hymn as she pulled it from the stone. The sterling blade felt right in her hands.

She turned to the white wolf. There was a look in its raging sea storms, not of pride but honour. It stalked the area around her, getting into a low stance. A snarl hung on its bared teeth. As tradition mandated, to christen a new blade wielder, it must spill blood within twenty-four hours of its new master. If not, then the blade is rendered cursed. She knew the tradition of human swordsmanship. This was no simple wolf. Esta believed it was the spirit of Sephril himself, which, ironically enough, is whom the white wolf references in human culture.

She flourished the light blade in her hands and readied for the wolf to pounce. Lightning crackled out of its eyes and its snarling maw of razor-sharp teeth. Fierce predatorial intent sent shivers of fear up the half-elf's spine. Tightening her grip with both hands, she readied for its attack.

At a breath's length, it leaped towards the seasoned half-elf warrior, causing her to tumble out of the way narrowly.

Recovering, she dodged the wolf's swipe and snatched her hand away in time not to have it become the wolf's snack.

Seeing an opening, she thrust her blade into the wolf's shoulder; a yelp escaped the old wolf. Retrieving her blade, the blood slowly dripped down its length and coated the runes inlaid on the sword's surface.

Esta recited in Diminaire, *"As sure as the drums of war strike true to the Song of War, so too shall this blade strike against my enemies and those that threaten my kin. Upon the blood spilled this day, may it be the last of innocents. It is my instrument of war. It is my tool of battle. It is my reaper of death."*

A roar twisted and gnarled as it interrupted all of creation itself. The two combatants halted in their dance of death as they heard the roar ring out. It belonged to no normal animal. It was almost insect-like as it lingered in the air.

They looked at each other, the wolf sat upon its haunches, and she watched as it dissipated. It slowly dissolved into thin air. It left behind something, however.

Before it fell into the murky water, she grabbed it. It was a thick white fur cloak made from the hide of a wolf.

"Thank you for finding me worthy."

Reality rushed back in as she donned the cloak and charged back into Alrizhod. Newfound determination coursing through her veins.

Chapter Fifteen: Sleep No More

Sana

What abomination is calling across creation? What beast of the night kept braying for the attention of the night's children? What creature rose to meet them?

They rushed through the streets, charging over the empty onyx stone of the streets beneath them that glinted in the moonlight. With each step, she could feel the hanging weight of the crown.

It felt hefty, the crown that hung upon her belt. Ever present was the question of whether to don it or not. It writhed in her mind like roiling ocean waves.

It spoke to her once more, *"If you don me, I can lead you towards something to give you an edge against the Skithik."*

The wayward Sanguinaire princess tucked that fact away, saving it for a later date. She had nothing to go off of if Drass spoke the truth. She hoped he did. If not, she would have nothing to prove her right to rule over her fellow Sanguinaire. The Sanguinaire, while by and large lawful, prize power. The Bellunaire, the non-elven vampires, more so than her Sanguinaire brethren. She knew how to win over her elven brethren. The Bellunaire embodied the more primal aspects of their blessing from Silthar; she needed something to prove that she could lead them. A question briefly lit her mind before she quickly tucked it away. Yet it lingered in the back of her mind all the same. Was she strong enough to lead?

Sana used her psychic connection to track where Esta was heading off to. Her sired ran towards what dark abomination awakened in the city's centre. Her head swirled with questions, threatening to overtake her actions. She pushed those thoughts back, whatever creature this was; Sana was sure Esta was not prepared to engage it.

Vedus roared over the whipping air as they charged through the streets of Alrizhod, "You go on ahead. I will meet you there."

Sana whipped her head around to meet Vedus as she said, "Vedus wait—"

However, he had already peeled away and disappeared into the strange geometry. She was impressed and likewise infuriated at how he could disappear like that. Each day he was growing in strength, whether by his own volition or not, but his power grew. She hoped that he could keep the whispers from the Queen of Shadows at bay; Sana heard rumours that only the strongest of wills could possess her power. She questioned the strength of a revivified prince that was haunted by the death of himself and his family could hold back the tide of bloodlust that lingered in the whispers of shadows.

None of that mattered as she halted at the steps of the ziggurat at the city centre. She looked over as she heard Esta approach as well. She held a new sword with a white wolf hide draped over her shoulders. Both of the new items were drenched in magical energy.

Esta connected her eyes to Sana and said in her mind, *"We have much to discuss after this."*

Sana nodded and looked at the dark creature that summoned them.

It was a towering humanoid abomination, insectoid in appearance. Plates of its chitinous exoskeleton were large enough to work as a full-body shield for a regular standing humanoid. It bore the colours of dark amber, its eyes a glowing purple, bursting with mist that was often a show of magical or psychic capabilities. Sana assumed the latter, considering that beasts like these tended to be in the small army of an Ilthaun cell. She had never known beasts like these to persist without a hivemind to keep them alive. Considering that it was not charging them immediately, that told Sana that it was debating whether or not to endanger the hive. She was slightly impressed that a hive could survive so long without fresh minds to enslave. She tucked away her questions as it shook with action, readying itself for a fight.

Her canines extended as she summoned a portion of her magical reserves; her vessel of magical energy was half-full. She hoped that it was enough to take on this abomination. She hissed at the creature, sending a message to the rest of the hive.

Unfazed, it roared again, reared up, and charged toward them. Its humanoid torso was perched atop a four-legged lower half. Wrapped in head to toe with its chitinous plates. Two oversized plates extended from its arms, acting as shields.

Shields raised as it neared Sana and Esta.

Sana charged as well, deciding to use her smaller size against it, and slid underneath its legs. She studied underneath its form while dodging the thick insect-like legs that threatened to crush her. It was as she suspected. It was nearly covered in thick plates.

She sprang to her feet after breaching the other side of the monstrosity.

Esta side-stepped, a strong horizontal slash connecting to one of its legs. While it was a strong strike, they both knew it to be a test stroke to see if the chitins could be easily broken. Not so.

Recovering with faster mobility than they both anticipated, whipping around and counter-charging them. As Sana dashed a few paces away, pulling in both hands, she unleashed a wave of crimson energy.

Travelling through the air, it burst as it struck the plates of the hulking beast, rattling it for a moment, but its shielded fists still cracked the obsidian stone beneath their feet.

Flicking her wrist, she summoned three darts of solidified scarlet energy. They all sailed through the air while they recovered from the strike upon the ground.

Two of them burst against the thick chitinous plate. A red mist spread over the large surface area of the plates. The third dart of energy found a gap in the plates. A loud hiss erupted from the wound, followed by a roar of pain.

It reared back and pulled its hands into the air, readying to connect its fists to the ground below.

Sana braced herself, but Esta charged forward after the shields slammed into the ground. A shockwave erupted across the obsidian floor underneath them. Sana wobbled, but she maintained her footing. Esta had already leaped into the air towards the abomination, sword poised and ready to strike.

She unleashed a quick flurry of slashes as she went through her arc. Each strike hit the chitinous plates, bar one that slid between the plates. A thick green ichorous fluid spilled forth from the fresh wound. Finding purchase upon the ground once more, she slid against the smooth surface.

Sana spoke hideous arcane verbs and bid her sword to come into existence once more, as her magical reserves were already almost depleted. She could feel the magical exhaustion weighing heavily on her, a distant ghost.

She launched herself into the fray as well. The two danced and exchanged blows against the plates of the beast as it slowly kept pace with them. The thick plates were harder than steel, which proved to have its advantage and the hive it served. Each moment they spent trying to bring this thing down was another moment that could bring another servant of the hive to them. Her anxiousness rose as the moments stretched on.

They did well enough to avoid being struck by its inhuman mandibles. Sana had been out of practice with her physical capabilities. However, she had found a rhythm that allowed her to keep herself safe and weaken the chitinous plates.

They found sync once more, and as they reeled back to strike, there was a brief moment where the only sound to be heard was the shrieking of the abomination they fought against.

Both of their blades pierced through the plate that covered its abdomen. A sickening crunch engulfed the air around them as they severed into its body.

However, Sana could not wrench her sword free, and neither could Esta. In a quick movement, she let her sword dissipate into thin air and dashed away from the hulking nightmare. She looked back from a safe distance and saw Esta as she struggled to rip her sword free from the creature.

Sana shouted, "You haven't bound yourself to the weapon! Do it now!"

Esta scrambled and pressed her palm against the surface of her blade. Using a different dialect of arcane language, the runes livened with activity. It accepted the ichorous blood as an offering.

As the brief ritual finished, she watched the sterling silver blade engulfed in shadow flame, choking the silver appearance and morphing it into a polished obsidian surface. The runes glowed a dark red that matched the hilt. She was not fast enough to let go of the blade and caught one of the shields as it flailed to try and harm whatever struck it.

Esta had taken the brunt of the strike, skidding against the ground. She seemed to be adapting to her vampirism well enough. Sana was glad about that. Flicking her wrist, she summoned her blade once more, and in a diagonal slash, she unleashed a concentrated wave of crimson as it collided against the chitinous shields. It exploded with a thunderous crash, awakening the long-dead city. Sana felt the explosion's aftershocks as it rolled off the beast.

Taking advantage of the newly formed weak point, she looked to Esta, who had a proud and fierce look on her face; she had not seen such confidence in Esta. For the longest time, she knew her as a fellow slave. She could now be proud to call her the Left Hand of Silthar.

Sana raised her dark blade, leaping back into action, and in a brief bright red flash, the beast was blinded and reeled back. Sana connected her sword against the soft spot they had exposed. Covering her in dark green ichor.

As it connected with her skin, she felt it singe slightly. Being a vampire had perks, one of them being a slight acidic resistance. Unfazed by this, they both unleashed their assaults of unrelenting ferocity. Ichor sprayed and coated everything in its thick viscous bile. Its limbs curled as life was pulled from it, like a spider gasping its last breath. The ground rumbled as it fell into a lifeless pile. Sana's breaths were long after the adrenaline slowly dissipated. Distantly, she could hear the coming steps of other servants of the hive. Raising her sword, she looked to Esta as she flicked her blade to clean it. The shadows that wreathed her blade fell, and she formed the shadows and changed their shape. Joining her cage-shaped hands together, the shadows were alight with bright red energy and eldritch intent.

Chapter Sixteen: Children of Delight

Vedus

The warping geometry nearly drove Vedus more insane than the powers threatening to overtake him. His mind slipped further with each passing moment. The voices grew louder and more antagonistic. He could hear the sound of Vastra in her mind.

"They think you're weak. They want to tear you limb from limb. They think you are not a worthy vessel for my mother's power."

The shadows took shape in the formless writhing mass of twisted geometry. Each step was long as he slowly but surely stopped in his tracks to the lashing forms within the shadows. They took the shapes of men and women around him, churning in a sea of formless bodies. A mass of flesh that rose and fell like the ocean tides. Some were strong enough to pull themselves out of the mass of flesh. Still taking the forms of women, their eyes were glossed over, a sickly opaque liquid with no coloration and no pupil to speak of. They lumbered, and as they came closer, reality shifted again.

Four of them surrounded him, wrapped in thin gowns of an opaque cloth, each laying their hands upon him, pawing and moving their hands over his form. He dared not move. They already kept him from moving. They had skin similar to that of Vastra, a dark blue that gave them the appearance that there was no blood flowing through their veins.

A new voice rose in his head, *"Do you like them, prince? They seem to enjoy your company."*

Struggling to maintain his composure as they continued to probe their hands over his form, his sanity and willpower tested, "Who… are… you? What do you… want?"

One of them piped up, "We only want to please you."

Another, "Are we not enough?"

A third, "We beg of you, please."

The voice rose in his head, *"They are yours. They are lost souls given to me from my warlocks, cambions they are called. They are stripped of what humanity is left, all except for lust and pleasure. They are my Children of Delight. And they are your servants. Introduce yourselves to him."*

The voice paused, allowing Vedus to absorb the information so far. They pulled at him, causing him to fall to his knees. They took turns drawing their attention to him.

The first had blonde, almost platinum hair. She smiled as she said, moving his head to his right to meet eyes, "I am Salaia."

The next, shifting his attention to Salaia's right, she had short black hair and said, "I'm Dalia."

The third shifted his attention towards her to the left. She had curly, auburn-colored hair and said, "My name is Savine."

The last, cupping her hands over his cheeks and drawing his attention to his far left, had long black hair pulled back into a ponytail. She seemed to have a more glossed-over expression, locked in a perpetual state of bliss. She had a smile that matched all the others and said, "My name is Vellia."

They all were pleasing to look at. He could feel himself losing focus and his willpower waning. They bore similar sculpted forms, lithe but slightly muscular. He could feel his mind fall into a deep haze. It could have been their collective lust that choked the air itself, though he was certain that it was the work of some spell or magical aura that engulfed him.

Dalia pressed herself against him, "We are ready to serve you in any way you see fit."

Salaia piped up next, drawing her fingertips over his chest, and said, "Whatever you want, we are yours."

The voice rose once more in his mind, *"Your first trial has been completed. The shadows seem to agree that you might prove worthy of wielding my power."*

This caught him off guard. He mused, "I could almost be certain they were growing more hostile."

"They were testing your will. Being a prince, you should know that power is not so easily wielded without some form of test."

His cloudy mind cleared for a moment, and one question arose in his mind with pure, driven purpose and fervour: as soon as it came to him, he said aloud, "Why was I resurrected? Why was I cheated of my death?"

His answer did not come as fast. He sat there waiting patiently as his cambions continued probing over his form. Her hands now slipped underneath some of his leather and armour. They cooed and giggled amongst themselves. They seemed quite content.

The voice said, *"You can thank your father for that. He made a pact with me to have himself and you be given life once more. I, for one, am fond of family bonds, not to mention the driven nature of revenants. I took pity upon your family's plight, plucked away from your lap of luxury by a greedy general with nothing but a thirst for war and blood."*

Vallia frowned and said, "It's not fair."

Dalia joined her and said, "You *poor* thing."

The voice continued, *"Your father did not make it past the first trial and has been driven mad by the whispers of the darkness. They did not like him. But you—"*

She paused and let the cambions speak for her. Dalia continued, "You proved to have a strong will and to carry yourself with such power."

Ecstasy's eyes were half-lidded as she said huskily, "So much power."

Salaia continued, "The voices were a test, and you passed."

Savine pushed him back, and he fell entirely against the ground. With just enough force that it did not hurt as much, she leaned in close and whispered, "We are your reward. So long as your pact remains true, we are yours to serve."

The voice rose one last time as she said, *"Take a moment. Enjoy your victory, Prince Vedus. Allow my Children of Delight to serve your every desire.*

I look forward to seeing how well you do on your next trial."

They all giggled, the pleasure was becoming too much, or something within him slipped into oblivion. A part of his soul was shaved off, disappearing into the void as they started to remove his armour and weapon. Lust-filled expressions overtook all of them. Desire raged like bonfire in their eyes. Vallia herself seemed more so than the others. His mind slipped into the void as they removed their gowns and began their reward for him.

Vallia leaned in and whispered, "You must kill Sana."

***

Vedus awoke, slowly opening his eyes. Lifting his torso as he pushed himself up.

He was sore. He looked around as his armour was laid strewn about along with his sword. This confirmed that what happened was not just some hallucination. It was real. His soul belonged to the Queen of Shadows. He felt a new weight upon his wrist, he looked, and it was a silver bracelet. It was four interwoven silver wires that wrapped snugly over his wrist. Representing his given servants from the Queen of Shadows, no doubt.

He quickly donned his armour and sword as he continued through the twisting streets.

Winding his way, he found what he had been searching for. In the bowels of a ruined armoury, he saw the armour.

Twisted and malformed steel wove around in hideous ways resembling an insect's armour. It appeared almost demonic though he felt no such diabolic aura emanating from it. Instead, it gave off an aura of reserved malice. Not towards him, which he considered a good thing.

Careful to not disturb some resting spirit, he equipped the twisted armour and could feel the psychical dampening begin to take hold. When he strapped on the last piece, the breastplate, he could for once feel absolute silence.

No whispers or murmurs in the darkness, just his thoughts. He hoped this would prove helpful in his trials ahead to gain further favour with the Queen of Shadows. She was a god. He felt assured that it could not psychically dampen her from his mind.

Drawing his fingers over the contorted steel, eying the bracelet he had been given, he thought to himself.

"How mad have I become?"

Flexing and moving around, he familiarised himself with the weight. He could hear the braying of the mighty abomination that called them into the city centre.

Pulling himself into the shadows, his formless shadow moved with blinding speed.

***

He leaped from the shadows and collided with one of the hostiles. It was a grey-coloured humanoid, wrapped in armour similar to his but evidently far less hardened as his sword cut cleanly through the soft chitin-like armour.

He seems to be the last one amongst his companions.

Vedus flourished his blade and looked at his vampire companions.

Despite her unamused look, Sana breathed evenly and said, "I would prefer if you did not leave like that; we could have used your help against that."

She pointed next to her to the bleeding mass of chitinous plates. Esta mirrored a similar disappointed look and said, "Where did you find that armour?"

Vedus countered, "Where'd you find that sword and cloak?"

Esta raised a finger in protest, but her words died in her throat as she said, "Fair point."

Sana motioned to the entrance to the ziggurat, "They seem to be coming from that. The previous hive that inhabited this city seems to be within that ancient temple."

Vedus nodded to the entrance as he sheathed his sword, "Then let's waste no more time.

Chapter Seventeen: Mind's Rend

Esta

As Vedus struck flint against the shadowed wall and lit his torch, Esta stalked with her sword drawn at the ready to strike. A bright scarlet emanated from the runes that ran the length of the blade. Sephril, she believed, was no longer an appropriate name. A presence made itself aware in her mind, but not like the psychic thoughts Sana would send to her. Its thoughts were empty, but its emotions were lively and raged like a fire. She could feel the breadth of its emotions in her mind because of its intensity. Esta decided to name it Blacksun.

They descended a staircase that ran down along the perimeter of the squared temple. The staircase was wide enough for one person with no railing on the left side, only a ledge that led to a quick death.

Brushing her hand against the wall, the eons-old stone, untouched by time, was soft and accepted her young fingers upon its antediluvian surface.

With a still breath, she said aloud, "What ancient horrors await us?"

Sana spoke up, her words almost a whisper upon the vast darkness that swallowed them as they descended the stairs. "An Elder Hive, from eons before the Revelation. They will shake us. Test our psyches in more ways than we thought possible. Keep your wits about you."

Was it a fool's errand, gathering information and tools needed to bring down the Skithik? Were they beyond their depth? These were questions she had reserved, questions that she dared not ask herself or out loud. Speaking from the mind brought fate to give life to your woes and fortunes.

Her thoughts wandered back to only a few hours ago when the world was black, and her arm was severed.

"Sana."

Getting her attention, she sighed, "Yes?"

Esta continued, "We are the Hands of Silthar, I have come to terms with that, but in the future, I would prefer to be more informed about what I have to face."

Sana struggled to find an answer, "Well... I—"

"You knew that I would need to struggle against hunger. I thought it was the hunger alone, but it's more than that. Some dark presence that mimics life that's slowly trying to overtake my mind, and you felt it appropriate to keep me from knowing that? Why?"

"Because you weren't ready," The Sanguinaire answered, keeping her composure as they walked. "You were still rejecting the gifts of Silthar; you still believe it to be a curse despite what it has given you so far."

Esta stopped in her tracks, raising her hand against Sana, and fed from the anger that roiled off of Blacksun as she said, "You believe me unworthy?"

"That is not what I said. What I said was—"

Esta grabbed her by the coat cuff and slammed her into the wall. Not enough to hurt, but enough to get her point across.

Vedus halted and said, "Esta *don't*—"

"Stay out of this, Vedus," she barked, looking at him as he sighed and watched the formless shadows in front of him.

She returned her gaze to Sana. There was no fear in her eyes. She growled, "We have had equal amounts of time in our positions, do not feign superiority when we both—"

Sana gripped her arm and squeezed with great force. Her strength was greater than Esta's, her bones relenting under the titanic grip as she said, "I never claimed to be superior. I never deemed myself more worthy of our positions. Silthar claimed us as his hands. If anything, we are equals."

They let go of one another, brushing herself off. Sana continued, "It's clear to me why you were chosen as well. But you are still young, the blessing of Silthar has set in, but you must learn to control the intense emotions that arise. There is never a time when you cannot temper your emotions."

Esta furrowed her brow, "You want me to detach myself?"

Sana sighed, "No, I did not say that, Alca—Esta. I said to temper your emotions. Anger, fear, passion, all of these emotions are amplified because of the blessing we have been given. Sangilis, the spirit of vampirism, the unhallowed spark of eldritch energy that keeps us alive, is a wild and untamed soul of emotion. It rages like a tempest, and we must control it. Not to detach ourselves, but to shave off the intensity."

Sana stepped closer, raising Esta's chin to meet their eyes. Her eyes were inviting, giant suns of a deep crimson hue. In the eyes of a mortal, they would be beguiling. "I failed to prepare you in the past, and you almost lost your life because of my ignorance, and for that, I am sorry. I cannot do this going forward."

Resting a hand on Esta's shoulder, she said, "I will guide you and help you control your blessing."

Her anger subsided, accepting Sana's words. Her eyes took her in as she had done many times before. She calmed her Sangilis, as Sana referred to it. She looked deeper into Sana's eyes. She felt that minor rivalry shaved off, all previous hatreds dimmed, and she saw something that she never thought she would see, mentorship.

Bringing Esta out of her eyes, Sana laid a hand upon her diaphragm and said, "I officially brand you as one of my sires. I shall guide you through the darkness and the hysteria."

They stayed there for a moment until Sana pulled back and motioned for them to continue. Esta was unsure what had changed, but she buried it for another day as they continued down the stairs in silence.

***

As they reached the bottom, the walls were covered in ancient murals of legends immortalised from the Divine Era. The first they saw was the Binding of Chaos when the Primordial Ones were locked away in the stars. The Shattering of the Infinite, when Xar'Loth severed the Infinite Planes and created the now twenty-four planes of existence before his millennia of imprisonment. The Founding of the Pantheons, when the Chaos of Light and the Chaos of Shadow claimed their entities for their respective pantheons.

Esta knew these tales from the priests of Uthos that would give sermons about the triumphs of the Pantheon when she served in the Eternium's army during the Olkhan Invasion. Though she knew of their existence, she cared not to believe his sermons. She did not have the same faith as her brother Ezran. They had Uthos to bring them to his afterlife. A half-elf like herself did not have such a luxury.

What was odd was that the murals were found in the bowels of an Ilthaun colony. Why would they commemorate the triumphs of a Pantheon they did not belong to?

Vedus mused, "Why would the Ilthauns make a mockery of these events?"

Sana answered, "These aren't mockeries. Just as the Dragons were the first servants of the Gods, the Ilthauns were the first servants of Chaos. Before the Demons and Devils spawned from the hideous blood of Korodon. Somewhere along the timeline, I am not sure when they separated from their masters and joined the ranks of the Void Pantheon. That is why they have such twisted complexions because they betrayed the forces of Chaos and accepted their new masters, the Elder Ones."

Esta looked around the magnificently carved stone murals. They were impeccable. To have such beauty come from twisted and corrupted people was beyond what Esta could envision. Perhaps they were not all monsters; perhaps Esta should not be one to judge them all as having one singular mindset when she would say the same about the vampires and herself. She still hated it, just as she still struggled to maintain the Sangilis. She could feel it pawing at her mind threatening to overtake her. With each breath, she pushed against it, drawing it back to a more resting state.

They walked through the maze-like halls of the temple in Alrizhod. The walls were damp and cave-like, but there was a carved nature about it that told her it was not such an easy feat to make the halls of the temple. Stonework, especially one that boasts intricacy rivalling the Dwarves, was never an easy thing to do. She wondered if it was the slaves that carved the murals and the immaculate stone tunnels of the temple or if it was the work of the Ilthauns themselves.

Esta did not know what they were looking for, and nothing was clear to her beyond the fact that the hive was awakened and knew of their presence within the city. The tunnels that accepted their forms were wide and tall enough to fit giants. From Esta's best guess, they were around eight metres tall by six metres wide. Carved and shaved to a smooth surface, the tunnels and floors flowed into one another, taking on the appearance of either a spiral or a circle. Whatever it was, something within Esta told her to be awestricken. The Ilthauns kept many slaves; they enjoyed their twisted menagerie.

They surmised the tunnels ran through the length and breadth of the city and then some. Where it all led to was uncertain. It all seemed to twist and wind its way back to one another.

The skittering of claws jolted them all from their focused states and plunged them into the mindset of battle.

Flourishing her blade, Blacksun ignited with a life eager to tear flesh. Vedus did the same, and Sana flicked her hands, igniting with magical life. They skittered closer, their forms now visible. They were vaguely humanoid that ran on all fours, wrapped around their eyes and their head was a spiked iron circlet. Mirroring the circlet, similar ones were wrapped around their wrists, ankles, upper arms, stomach, and chest. They wore no armour other than that; their teeth filed to fine-edged points.

Just before they came within two metres of them, they simultaneously screeched. Esta reeled back, feeling an assault upon her mind. It felt as though a hideous spike struck itself into her head, her vision blurred for a moment, unable to process the attack. The assault upon her mind felt continuous.

Before she could recover, she felt a force bash against her knocking her to the ground. She maintained a firm grip on her sword and retrieved from the pushback. Sliding against the circular floor, she raised her sword as she felt the air shift with a dashing opponent. It unknowingly glided through the extended sword, a gasp and screech releasing from its doomed form. Mortality slipped from its eyes.

Her crimson-stained blade hovered over the slumped form on the ground, leeching the bleeding essence from the now-dead combatant. It fed her blade as well as herself, she had only known the taste of blood, but the taste of ancient magical essence was something she could get used to. Using some of the stolen essences, her eyes lit up with a dark red glare, flaring like raging suns. Her mind cleared from the psychic assault she had been suffering. She surveyed the area around her.

Sana was handling herself well, spell after spell slung from her off-hand; the other often carried the shadow blade she summoned for combat.

Vedus struggled to maintain his psychic defences as three of them predatorily encircled him, assaulting and pulling apart his mind. Using a portion of the stolen essence, she flicked her hand into the air as she whispered a hideous sound. The air crackled with life as a concentrated ball of scarlet essence launched into the air and landed in the space shared by Vedus and the three skittering dooms.

It faded from existence for a moment and then erupted in deep crimson light. The dark red energy took the form of vines and wrapped around the three servants of the hive. She charged them as they struggled to loosen themselves from their bonds. They all lashed out in a last-ditch effort. She felt her shielding against the psychic energies wane for but a moment. Pain slivered in, and she felt a spike of energy pierce through her mind and rend into her thoughts. She howled in pain as she severed their mortal essences from their bodies.

Drawing in their essences, she pressed her hand against Vedus's head, healing what damage had been done and coating his mind in a layer of defence. Hers cracked from the simultaneous assault; helping him back to his feet, she could hear more of them coming. She did not know how many more assaults like that she could take, but she was damned if she did not try. Her eyes and blade flashed with life, hideous intent imprinting upon her foes.

Chapter Eighteen: The Right to Rule

Sana

Sana's shadow blade sliced through flesh as if she was harvesting wheat. With each bloody servant of the hive that fell, she used the mortal essence to embolden her psychic defences. While they only used one psychic technique, they were well-versed in using it. In terms of the official curriculum of the Zarlonian wizards, the technique was called Carnage of Mind. It was a form of magic that, if left unprotected, could cause brain haemorrhaging. Yet because the Archmages forbid psychic magic, Sana only knew the four techniques of psychic magic and how to defend against it. It would not be long before her magical reserves forsook her.

The stench of bile and blood filled the chamber they fought within. She lost count of how many rose to face her; thirty had fallen between Esta, Vedus, and herself. More still came, their maddening claws scraping against the rugged stone that encircled them. They climbed all over the walls, their hunched forms frightening her.

Sana tried to reach out and find the hivemind's centre, where the Elder One or Ilthaun resided. Yet the barriers remained in place, and each time she tried to reach out, there was only a sea of blank memories to sift through, like wading through thick fog with no light. She ceased as her shadowed blade glided across the neck of another slave to the hivemind. Drawing the mortal essence and applying another layer, she considered something that had been bothering her. Originally, the hivemind sent a monstrosity to meet them. It was an attempt to either make them flee or kill them outright. She found it strange that they would send servants so weak to face them.

It dawned on her, her eyes growing wide as she summoned all the magical strength she could and erected a force barrier between them and the servants of the hivemind.

Vedus and Esta looked over to Sana, who shouted, "These are a distraction! We have to run!"

As she finished, they heard a thunderous reptilian roar. Sana listened to a sound similar to that only once. She felt goosebumps form over her as fear rose in her throat to strangle any words before they left her lips. Beyond the incessant pounding of the mind slavers, they saw a monstrous shadow take shape a half-mile away. It sauntered on four limbs; they could feel the pounding as it slowly approached them. As it came closer, it took shape.

The creature had no wings but a mass of black scales that ran the length of its form. Its reptilian eyes glowed the same purple as the monstrosity they killed. Pieces of its flesh appeared to almost peel from its form. Its eyes flashed, and the mind slavers ceased their attack. It lifted itself, standing upon its hind legs. The air rippled as it snarled, clutching its clawed hand in the air. The magic of her barrier strained under its grip.

Its voice spoke, chorused by thousands of others, "You are unwelcome here, remain, and you will die. Flee, and you might yet live."

Sana held her hands out to reinforce the barrier, looking at Vedus and Esta, who froze in their place. They were gripped by fear and the aura of dread that rolled off its cursed shoulders.

Esta choked. "What in the name of the Pantheon is that?"

Straining, Sana replied, "Either this is the avatar of the hivemind, or it *is* the hivemind. Though I have never known or read of any dragon that became a hivemind."

"I am Kyz'uloth. First of my kind to fall to the temptations of the Endless Ones. Heed my warning or face annihilation."

There was no hope for them. All they could do was delay the inevitable. Only one thing was certain.

Sana broke the barrier and resummoned it behind her. Esta and Vedus were plunged from their stupor and saw what she was doing. Esta bashed a fist against the barrier and shouted, "Sana! What are you doing?"

Sana breathed, certain this was the only way they could escape. She took the crown off her belt and said, taking in the ancient weight of magic that lay within it, "Run. I will buy you both some time."

She looked directly at Esta. She could see tears start to form in her eyes. "Never falter and never yield to the Sangilis. You bring the Sangilis to face your enemies. Never succumb to despair lest you lose yourself to its madness."

A tear ran down her cheek. Vedus put a hand on her shoulder and forced her to follow him. It pained Sana to see her in such a state, just as they were moving past their rivalry and now this.

She heard Esta's voice in her mind. *"You can't...."*

"It's the only way. Flee—free our people. Protect Vedus. But most of all, kill the Skithik."

Sana looked to the iron crown in her hands and whispered, "Silthar, protect me and guide them to safety."

She lowered the crown unto her head, and as it rested upon her brow, she felt the air warp around her.

Drass rumbled in her mind. Deep satisfaction purred upon his voice as he said, *"Yes. We shall do great things together. But first, to rid the world of a blight."*

The dragon said, "What is this?"

Sana and Drass answered in unison, "Your *doom*."

Chapter Nineteen: Vengeance of Aeons

Drass

Shaking the dust of time, Drass's cursed mind extended into reality once more, renewed by the acceptance of Sana Nailo, who resided comfortably in the back of her head. Only for a few moments, he hated the physical world. After residing within the physical plane for so many millennia, he grew bored with the innumerable amount of disappointments brought to life in the world that felt estranged to him.

Neither Drass nor Kyz'uloth moved. Tendrils of psychic energy clashed in the air between them. Drass sneered as he seized control of the mind slaves. For too long, Drass had waited for this, to wipe the corrupted dragon from this plane. The dragon had no right to take what was his. Fresh in his mind was the image of the dragon devouring his Elder One.

For so many thousands of years, he slumbered with independence, with freedom from any hivemind. It felt strange and torturous to be without purpose, to exist within the confines of an iron prison. He made it in hopes of a tribal human taking it up so he could overtake their mind, but when none came, he felt despair. Death did not linger on his fate, the spectre of otherworldly judgement. Now he would be Kyz'uloth's executioner.

The dragon smiled. "You have survived after all these years."

"I am not so easily killed, Kyz'uloth."

The dragon lowered his head threateningly, its eyes wreathed in the purple flame, the sign of his former Elder One that lingered within the contents of Kyz'uloth's mind, and the blighted dragon said, "So it would seem. I always secretly hoped that you persisted after so many centuries so I could kill you myself, and there would be no hope of a rebellion of my servants against me."

Drass read the minds and memories of the enslaved surrounding him, ready to fight and die for him against their tyrant. They were vampires, yet fed upon psychic energies rather than blood. These were the wayward souls of the Skithik, the supposed masters of blood that reigned with an iron fist on the island of Urstron.

He sent them away, and they scuttled back into the shadows that spawned them—straightening his back and standing defiantly against the towering image of Kyz'uloth that was only a few feet away.

Its eyes were fierce and sinister. The promise of bloodshed leaked from its eyes as it said, "No pawns?"

Drass shook his head, "No such satisfaction. Their purpose is not done."

Kyz'uloth smiled. "I will enjoy this."

Drass unleashed a tidal wave of psychic energy against the dragon. "As will I."

***

For hours they fought, attempting to break each other's wills, severing connections, and destroying memories. They wore at each other until only husks remained. Once nearly every shred of memory that made them who they were had burnt away, they finally resorted to physical blows.

Though Drass was out of practice, he held his own against Kyz'uloth's titanic form. He was much faster, yet Kyz'uloth's power would easily best him if it got a clean strike.

He knew the dragon had poisoned claws, so potent that even Sana's vampiric regeneration could not withstand it. Undoubtedly, Kyz'uloth's tools for enslavement. Drass's plan was formulated as he dodged and weaved the broad swipes of the dragon that wanted nothing more than to tear him into shreds.

He slid underneath the dragon and summoned Sana's shadow blade as he glided across the uneven floor. The unbalanced sword pierced through corrupted flesh, black ichor spilling out of a wound that ran the length of its belly.

It would not last long, but it would distract him long enough to work.

Drass reached out to the minds of the psychic vampires. Some barriers kept their identities and their psychic abilities at bay. He could feel them festering, writhing with agony as they tried to break the locks free. However, these locks came with a price. Kyz'uloth was clever. The only way to unlock them was by sacrificing a portion of psychic energy. As much as he hated that fact, he saw no other way to finish this.

In a blink, he sacrificed nearly all of his psychic capabilities to unlock their minds. Kyz'uloth felt this, smiled as the wound began to heal, and began to tear flesh and warp his mind as he turned slowly. "Why sacrifice your power?"

Drass struggled to maintain his grip upon reality, struggling with every ounce he had left, and said, "I want to die… but not before I take *you* with me."

Kyz'uloth's eyes burned with patient fury, unfolding the mental assault he unleashed upon Drass. Bracing himself, he could feel every part of him slowly peel away from reality. His purpose, identity, and thousands of years of memory; evaporated instantly. Large gaps, where everything that made him who he was, only emptiness remained. He no longer registered pain, set adrift in a world that truly forgot him. All that remained was his name and his hatred for Kyz'uloth.

Drass breathed heavily as he struggled to replace what was lost, filling in the gaps. He shot his head up and saw Kyz'uloth reeling back and writhing in agony.

Kyz'uloth swore and shouted, "If I am going to die, then you're coming with me."

As he unleashed a psychic assault, Drass instinctively countered, and the opposing forces collided. Tendrils of psychic energy vied for control of each other's minds, shredding them apart.

Kyz'uloth screamed as the air around him warped. He slowly began to disappear and peel from reality. Drass's counterassault was just enough for the dragon to start dissipating from reality. Piece by piece, he was being torn from all planes of existence. All memories of him would die, all notions that spoke of him, gone.

Drass limped towards him, staying behind the psychic assaults of the mind slaves, and watched with joy as his sworn enemy for countless millennia was now being torn to shreds by the psychic vampires.

All was dust when it was said and done, and with that, Drass's vengeance was complete. Satisfied, with fractions of his psyche remaining, he fell back into the recesses of Sana's mind and pulled Sana back into her body.

"I am done. I can now rest that my sworn enemy is dead. I do not know if your body will survive the ordeal I put it through, and I am sorry. I am fulfilled and return you to your place in the world. I pray for your survival, Hand of Silthar."

Chapter Twenty: The Rebellion of Night

There was no pause for respite, no time to reflect upon what had been done. Esta and Vedus burst out into the land above and saw torchlights surrounding the city. Rain fell with severe hatred, and a thin mist covered the city. The sound of vampires rose high in the rainfall, their primal hissing and moans of agony. The Skithik, likewise, growling orders to the vampires and themselves.

Unsheathing Blacksun, fury rose in Esta's eyes. "Kill as many as you can. Free the vampires."

Vedus unsheathed his sword and said, "But what about—"

"We can mourn the loss of Sana later. Now we prepare for war!"

Esta charged forward and leaped from the last stair, her sights set upon two unsuspecting Skithik.

Her blade glided through their flesh with such ease that her sword sang with joy as it tasted upon the blood of the Skithik. Leeching the essence and feeding Esta as well, she delighted in the slaughter.

In a fluid slash, she decapitated the other Skithik, and with her off-hand, she willed the blood that resided within it to bend to her will. All ten pints of blood drained from the Skithik and succumbed to her mind.

She willed the blood into tiny needles as the vampires swarmed around her, gnashing their sharpened teeth with animalistic hatred. She sent all the needles out, and rather than puncturing the vampires, they found the scarabs that caused them to follow the orders of the Skithik obediently. They reeled back simultaneously and recovered from the months of rehabilitation.

Esta raised her voice high for all to hear, all thirty of them, "Listen to me now, brothers and sisters of Silthar. Long have your thoughts and actions not been your own, for you have been imprisoned by the treacherous slavers of Urstron. To live and die at their command.

"But Silthar himself has named me one of his Hands. And he has called for a rebellion against these traitors of the night. They break, beat, and bend you to their will. No more. Now is the time that we take back what is our right. Now we take back the night and its glorious splendours. For this night, we shall feast upon their blood and show them that the servants of Silthar shall not KNEEL!"

She thrust Blacksun into the sky and shouted for all to hear, "FOR SILTHAR! FOR FREEDOM!"

They cried out in agreement and hissed as the Skithik slowly began gathering outskirts of the city centre. Esta moved her hate-filled scarlet eyes upon them, her sword remaining high in the sky, and whispered to herself, "For Sana...."

Lightning struck the black stygian metal and flowed through her. She changed the nature of its damaging energy, and with her outstretched hand, she let the lightning burst from her fingertips. She struggled to maintain the flow but dug her heels into the stone and maintained focus. Her Sangilis held the reckless power at bay as tongues of electricity burst forth.

Red tongues of lightning burst from her fingertips and struck five of the approaching Skithik, jumping from one target to the next. As it stopped on the fifth, their forms burned, and their flesh sloughed off their bones. Their prideful eyes burst from the force that ran through their veins. As the fifteen vampires they commanded began to charge, she willed the blood of all five of the ruined Skithik to destroy their scarabs.

She shouted, "Go, free your brothers and sisters of the night! And leave none of the Skithik alive. Tonight, we dine on their blood!"

They went forth, taking up weapons strewn by the Skithik and what they could find in the city's houses, which was little more than table knives. Two of them scrambled to her, a human male with ragged blond hair and a stern form. The other was a half-orc, its charcoal skin and small tusks protruding from his mouth. Their scarlet eyes looked upon her with purpose.

The human bowed and said, "I am Gethin, and this is Korugul. We are yours to command."

Esta nodded and said, "I am Esta Desidarius. We must find the armoury and give them the weapons and armour they need to survive. You two will aid me in this endeavour. I fear they will not last long without it."

They both nodded, she walked past them, and as she began a fast jog, she said, "We are the Unshackled, and we shall be free of these Skithik."

Cries of vengeance and hatred filled the streets as the rebellion of the night began, and Esta was determined to wipe the Skithik from the face of Calisine. Upon the grave of Sana and the will of Silthar, she would lead this rebellion to victory against the Skithik and then find and kill the traitor

Enoch the Nocturnal. For now, they needed weapons and armour to last more than the night.

***

They scoured the streets, avoiding Skithik and the wandering eyes of enslaved vampires. She could feel the connection of forty-five of those she freed. She could feel their emotions, their actions, and their strength. Though they fed upon blood, they were still not up to strength to fight ever onward into the night. They needed to be armed and armoured.

Rounding a corner, the three of them entered a building, and as they crossed the threshold, they saw a Skithik in the centre. Black stone walls and ceilings did well to try and hide it, but their nightly vision could see him clear as day. The room was five metres long by three metres wide. From what Esta could tell, it was once a shop.

Leaping over the counter, the Skithik howled in anger as it charged them.

Esta did not move, she merely nodded her head towards him, and Korugul and Gethin counter-charged it, axe and sword respectively raised defiantly in the air.

They clashed with it for a moment, their stances were sloppy, and their strikes were wild, like children with sticks.

Uncoordinated and without proper discipline. She would need to remedy that in the future. But because they outnumbered him, Gethin got in a strike and punctured its neck.

As it reeled from the strike, Korugul let out a battle cry and embedded the axe into the Skithik's chest, puncturing the chest and severing several arteries from its heart.

Satisfied with their kill, she waved a hand and said, "Drink up. You'll need the strength. Find me when you're done. I will search for anything about an armoury."

Korugul answered for both of them and said with a nod, "At your command, Lord-Sire."

Esta stopped in her tracks for a moment, Lord-Sire. She enjoyed the sound of that.

She spent the next few minutes rushing through the shop and frantically searched for anything that mentioned an armoury. She found the office area and searched through ledgers for any mention of an armoury. Nothing. She went upstairs and scoured the rooms for letters but found nothing helpful.

Esta found the study adjacent to the master bedroom and found scoured maps. Searching through them, she found a map of Alrizhod. Scratches and marks were made upon it.

But what was important was that it was labelled and had a legend that pointed her to the armoury. Unfortunately, it was some ways away, in the ward opposite where they were.

Nodding, she grabbed the map, folded it, tucked it in her belt, and left the room.

As she stepped into the hallway, she heard the sound of Gethin and Korugul in the midst of a fight. She stepped and melded into a mist. The plumes of grey smoke burst through the air as she quickly made her way to the shop entrance.

When she made her way to the entrance, she saw two Skithik engaged in a fight with Gethin and Korugul. They held their own, but they would surely succumb to the superior technique of the Skithik.

She took form right behind them and, without them knowing, in one cleaving strike, severed the torso of one and embedded her sword into the side of the other. Straining with all of her might as her blade gladly tasted flesh and blood.

They fell to the ground with the lost mortal essence that gave them life.

Drawing their spirits and feasting upon their corrupted souls, Esta felt her strength grow. She straightened her back, she could feel her Sangilis writhing within her. It clawed against the bars of her soul, her tainted black soul that relished the bloodshed, that tasted sweet, the blood of those that opposed her.

Esta took a moment to reflect as she ordered Gethin and Korugul to follow her. Was she lost? Did she succumb to the Sangilis already without even knowing it? But she felt it was still locked within herself. Was it the fervour of vengeance?

She did not know, but one thing was sure; they were one step closer to an active rebellion. She could feel the freed minds of the lost vampires that raged through the streets. In time she would have them to be her sires, but for now, she would give them their teeth.

***

It was loud now, the surmounting rebellion that filled the streets of Alrizhod. Her forty-five vampires did well in their freeing of the enslaved vampires. She counted one-hundred and eighty-seven. A fraction of the vampires that were enslaved to the Skithik, but enough to cause trouble for them.

Crossing the city centre, they entered the ward upon the far side of where they came from. Their strides were long, stepping with the blessing of the night. She could feel the roiling strength within. Their strength was her strength. With each Skithik they killed, she could feel their strength grow and strengthen their sire to her. It was sweet, so many months of hatred towards what she was forced to be given.

The shame and guilt of her ancestral bonds hung over her head like an albatross.

She found strength in those around her; she relished in the binding of mind and actions to her. Lord-Sire Esta Desidarius was a name she could get used to. For once in what felt like a lifetime, she found an inner strength within herself. Though she still struggled with the Sangilis, she was proud of what she had become. She felt renewed. They were her new bloodline.

Esta flexed her left hand. All remnants of pain from when it was severed from her were gone. Whether from the time or her evolving strength, it was unclear what gave her arm such freedom.

They approached the armoury, the large circular building that was twice as large as many of the nearby buildings. It was there that their victory would be assured. But she felt something, a hideous aura that emanated from the building.

The Lord-Sire raised her hand and said, "Wait."

Gethin and Korugul halted, weapons ready to strike as they waited for further orders from their Lord-Sire.

Emerging from the armoury was a tall standing Skithik. A Skavarn warrior, the unmistakable white scales and red-tinged fins and eyes. Wrapped in glimmering silver armour, the shine from the metal alone lightly burned her skin and eyes. Flinching, she looked at the various heads wrapped around him, namely his belt and his over his shoulder.

His form was lighter than the other Skavarn she faced, not as monstrous.

A smile crossed its hideous reptilian maw as it said, "One of the Hands of Silthar. A blessing that I get the chance to kill you. Such a noble act, freeing your brethren from us. Indeed, but fruitless. We are but a scouting force. You will soon face the full might of the Skithik army."

Gethin and Korugul looked to her for orders. She lowered her hand they choked back their hisses and guttural growls towards the Skavarn.

In one fluid motion, she unclasped her cloak, and as it fell to the ground, the Skavarn spat, "You dare wear the skin of one of my brothers!?"

Flourishing Blacksun, the stygian metal singing hatred in the rippling rain-filled air as she cursed, "My blade will be my apology."

He hissed, "You may have slain Telarth, but I shall avenge him by spilling your blood!"

He charged, twin serrated bone daggers raised and ready to lacerate their flesh.

She sidestepped and, with both hands, brought down her sword in a quick slash, testing the reflexes of the Skavarn. He recovered quickly and countered with a flurry of strikes. He was quick, but she managed to dodge and weave around his viper-like speed.

As his daggers crossed, she ducked underneath them, getting herself closer, stepping within centimetres. He reversed the daggers and plunged them down. Resting the flat of her blade against her palm, she blocked the plunging promises of pain and misery.

Straining against his strength, she pushed them away and grabbed the unsharpened blade before thrusting deeply. Heat rolled off of his silver armour as he narrowly dodged impalement. Her blade tasted blood and relished in the howl of pain as it recovered from the strike.

As he stepped back, he got two quick slashes over her shoulders, where her arms met her torso. She grunted against the pain. She was stepping back as well.

Puzzled that her wounds were not closing, she heard a chuckle from the Skavarn as he said, "Your proximity to my armour stopped your regeneration; now *die*."

He unleashed another flurry of blows. With the wound she made, she could still draw small amounts of strength from him, but since he was a vampire like herself, there was not much she could gain from it.

These Skavarn always managed to keep her on her toes. They were not as wild as their Skithik brethren, that kept the vampires under control. He was too fast, and she did not have the time to keep making minor cuts against this well-trained warrior. There was only one way to end this, and she hoped her hunch was correct.

She lost steps with the Skavarn, and he swiped her sword away and brought her to her knees. He plunged his daggers into her chest, severing her breastplate, and she felt the daggers twisting their way into her flesh. Her breath caught in her throat, the blades gave a numbing sting as they embedded themselves into her.

Gethin and Korugul cried out and raised their weapons for a moment as they readied themselves to charge.

He twisted the daggers causing her to gasp in pain as she struggled to maintain consciousness; he cursed with a snarl, "Die, insolent wretch."

She remained there, her chest blazing with intense pain. Moments stretched on, and the raging skies above slowed their swirl. In the quiet, Esta reached out through her mind and said to the Lord of Bloodlines, *"I accept my place at your side."*

"May your bloodlines lend you strength."

She reached out to those sired to her, drawing upon their strength. Each of them felt this, and they willingly gave some strength. She thanked each of them as she drew upon the portions of their strength, and she could feel unlife filling her once more. So much so and to such a degree she could feel her veins flooding with power.

The Lord-Sire pushed against the strength of the Skavarn, and fear bled from his wide eyes as his strength dwarfed hers, which kept her at her knees. Wreathed in scarlet energy, she looked at the Skavarn in the eyes and said with a devilish smile, revealing her long canines, "I am one of the Hands of Silthar. My bloodlines give me strength. I am a vampire no more. I am an avatar of his power and will. And I find you unworthy of his blessing."

Gaping her mouth, she breathed in and drew upon the twisted curse that gave him his abilities. She watched as the colour ran from his face as she devoured the necrotic essence that gave him his vampiric gifts.

A husk remained, and she tossed it aside.

She wobbled to maintain her balance. Dizziness set in, Gethin and Korugul rushed to keep her up, and Gethin said, "Easy now, Lord-Sire."

She shook the dizziness from her head as she felt the wounds on her chest slowly heal. The flesh formed back into place as she said, "I'm fine. I'll be fine."

Shaking herself, she shot her head up as she heard in her mind, *"Only after I sacrifice myself do you finally accept your place at Silthar's side?"*

She wanted to weep with joy as she answered back, *"Sana?! I thought you were dead?"*

Esta swiveled her head around to try and find her, Gethin and Korugul were confused, and Korugul asked, "What is it? Is it another one of those Skavarn?"

She shook her head and said, "No, it is the other Hand of Silthar."

Gethin chimed in, "Where?"

Finding her gaze upon the temple in the centre of the city, she saw a figure cloaked in the night itself. Esta knew at that moment that Sana Nailo was no mere wayward princess of the Sanguinaire. No, she was the Heir of the Night. Wreathed in the silver light of the moon, she sent out her servants from the hive she destroyed.

She smiled and sent a message to all those sired to her to bring all of those they freed and themselves to her location to be properly fit for battle. The Children of Silthar will regain their place as the predators of the night. First the Skithik, then Enoch the Nocturnal.

Esta picked up Blacksun and entered the armoury, hungry for better armour.

Chapter Twenty-One: The Heir of the Night

Sana

Thrusting into her body, she sent out a small wave of magic that erupted in the air around her. Sending those around her back.

She cried out, "Stay back!"

"Stop. We do not wish to harm you."

She furrowed her brow as she opened her eyes, still within the confines of the tunnels beneath Alrizhod. The shadows lapped against her form, shrouding her in their forgiving embrace. Cooling her ragged muscles from the strain of the psychic forces she endured.

Holding herself firm, she looked over those that spoke to her. They were the hunched slaves of the hive that they were slaughtering no more than a few moments ago, which puzzled her. She tried to recall what happened, but all she got in return was a blur. She reached out to Drass and asked, *"What happened? What did you do?"*

He answered, *"I cleansed this place of the last shreds of the Elder One that I once called my master. These are psychic vampires that I freed from the bonds of Kyz'uloth."*

She nodded; addressing them, she said, "Who are you?"

In unity, they answered by gesturing to themselves. "We are Tantibrus. We are the last shreds of the Elder One that resided here. We must thank you for freeing us from the confines of the black dragon."

Breathing heavily, she said, "Yes… not an issue… forgive me, but I must ask, what will you do now?"

They looked at each other, confused, as they said, "We shall serve you."

"Me? Why me?"

"While we are Tantibrus, we still carry shards of our vampiric selves. Rather than feed upon blood and mortal essence, we feed upon thought and emotion. Our hive has been damaged, and there is no bother in returning to the wounded hive. So, we agreed to become sires to you."

Stunned, Sana reeled back and took it in. She recovered most of her mental strength, still taking in the information she had just received. How fascinating that vampires under such dire circumstances could alter their natures and change how they receive their strength. But the time to linger on this notion passed, and she could still feel the boiling emotions of Esta as she struggled to maintain her Sangilis.

She turned and went charging for the exit. Only to be stopped by Tantibrus, she growled, "As your Sire, I order you to let me by."

"Unfortunately, we are not your sires yet." They spoke earnestly. She had no notion that they were speaking out of anger or frustration, "We must endure a binding ritual if you recall correctly. We also have a gift for you."

Raising an eyebrow, she asked, "What kind of gift?"

They parted a few metres away and motioned her to follow them.

She nodded, and they guided her through the tunnels underneath Alrizhod. Tantibrus spoke, "For centuries, we ruled this city. Countless mortal generations pass within a blink of an eye. Millennia we slumbered under these stone streets and waited. Our vampire selves were freed from the bonds of the Skithik only to find the company of another more cruel slaver, twisting our minds and changing the nature of our being itself. Blood and mortal essence no longer became our source of strength, but thought and emotion replaced that hunger.

"Now that Kyz'uloth is dead, we can look to the future with you. This gift was given to our most decorated champion in our midst so many aeons ago. They fought with this armour in the wars from the Divine Era. The memories of war linger on it. It will give you strength."

For what felt like hours, they wound their way deep into the tunnels. They began to grow smaller, the geometry twisting and malformed again, though her eyes and mind had grown used to it.

They were deposited into a stone chamber a kilometre in diameter. Twisted stone stairs rose from a wreathing pool of water as it rose high, nearly touching the ceiling a kilometre high. Upon a stone, wrack was armour, veiled in light that shafted from a small hole in the ceiling.

Tantibrus said, "The Armor of Logal, the previous bearer of its power. It will bond with you, amplifying your psychic and magical abilities. It will be a great weapon in your crusade against the Skithik and the rebel lord of Silthar."

Sana turned and said, "How do you know about that?"

They answered, "Drass informed us of your plight, and we will serve you in whatever way possible."

They paused as they motioned to the armour and said, "Take it. And claim the power of mind and magic."

Walking each step to the armour felt like a lifetime, the ancient energy that presided within the armour warped the area around it, distorting what she could have seen. As she climbed the stairs, two things happened.

One, she could feel every decision she made leading her to this moment. Every action, every inaction, every time she told the truth, and every time she told a lie. It led her to this moment when she would claim the armour and take up her true birthright. All those years ago, she heard her father tell her, *"There will be a day when I am no longer in power. When the night is cold, and Calisine writhes in the darkness for someone from the night to guide them. When our people are lost and without leadership. You will be the Heir of the Night; you will be the one to take up the mantle I leave behind."*

Sana said to herself, remembering the words she replied with on that day, "What if I'm not ready?"

She remembered his smile. *"No one is ready to rule, my daughter. The weight of leadership is not one that people carry lightly. Some are naturally fit to lead; others need guidance along the way. You are not alone. You have your family and your people at your back to guide you. They will tell you if you are doing your job right. All you need to do is lead with confidence and benevolence."*

The memory ceased. It was a simple lesson that she learned, and one she still struggled with to that very moment when she readied herself to take up the strange armour and grab hold of the power she needed to rule and lead her people against the Skithik menace.

The second occurred halfway up the steps. She could hear a council of voices discussing in her mind. One of them was stern and spoke with a raspy voice, *"So, another wishes to claim the armour?"*

Another piped up, their voice was thin and eked out with great resistance, *"Are they worthy of the power that resides within?"*

A third joined the conversion, ragged and painful. *"She carries the blessing of Silthar. I am inclined to believe they have the strength to take up the armour."*

A fourth voice that was strong and rumbled with cruelty in its deep voice, *"Too weak! She is too weak for the power that rests within."*

The first said again, *"Thousands of years with techniques and teachings from thousands of wielders preside within the armour. Magic and warfare blend with the teachings that reside within the armour. A learner could don the armour and be given the rank of both Archmage and General."*

The second voice hissed, and its airy voice strained. *"But all is lost if one is not prepared to undergo the mental strain of so much information rushing into their minds. It is enough psychic energy to boil one's brain. Leaving little more than a husk behind."*

The fourth barked, *"She will be consumed by the psychic energy. She is too weakened by the fight she endured. She will succumb to the energy that will test her mettle."*

The third interjected, *"She is the daughter of Silas Nailo, the Nine-Slayer. The Nightlord. The Black Prince. The Fallen One. Her teachings from her father alone are enough to prove her pedigree. Surely will she struggle to maintain the flow of information into her mind, perhaps? But she will survive as all of us did before. I am sure of this."*

She reached the top, a trapped wind echoing across the ancient stones as her last foot crossed the stone pillar's top.

Sana stared long at the armour. It was insectoid in appearance and would nearly cover every inch of her except at the joints. The plates looked beaten and dented, the surface rising and falling like the carapace of a scorpion. There was no helmet, as she suspected, considering the armour had Ilthauns in mind that very rarely wore helmets. But the twisted iron matched the turbid nature of her crown. Drass offered no words of wisdom other than silent approval.

Removing the rags she had worn for many days and her cloak of Skithik skin. She began the process of donning the armour. It was a long affair that lasted longer than she anticipated, but as she clasped the last bit of armour upon her, she felt it.

Her mind flooded with information, memories of war, and everything in between. The air distorted until her surroundings were no longer visible. Spikes of psychic energy impaled her mind and injected information.

She collapsed to her hands and knees, screaming as she dug her fingernails into the rock. The pain nearly caused her to blackout; each time she felt herself start to slip into unconsciousness, she fought back against it with her psychic capabilities. Each time she resisted, it returned with more power and necessity.

There was a break, and then she felt her veins lit aflame. It ignited with magic so ancient that it neared the magic of Chaos. It brimmed in her veins; her natural regeneration began its work healing the singed veins. It grew to a mere dull numbing sensation.

Sweat began to soak her muscles as she struggled through the first trial of donning the armour.

At once, both mind and body crept with numbing cold. The crippling despair of defeat spread across her veins and her mind. Spreading without abandon and pause, she nearly lost herself as she fought back, stopping mere centimetres before her entire body was wrapped in the frostbitten sickness. Screaming as she pushed the energy and feeling aside, the air erupted in the binding of soul and magic.

She was forever imprinted upon the armour as the armour was imprinted upon herself. It was armour no longer; it was her second skin. Rather than boil or fester with ice-cold energy, her veins brimmed with a power she was familiar with.

She breathed with ease as the binding ritual was complete. Her muscles felt lighter, and her mind sharper. Her vision cut through the warped air around her.

With a wave of her hand, she dismissed the curtain of distortion.

All of Tantibrus looked upon her and bowed. Brimming with power, she absorbed the magical energy and nearly became drunk on it.

She raised her hand as her mind stretched out as she saw Esta stabbed with twin daggers made of serrated bone, a hideous Skavarn chuckling as it killed its quarry. But she felt Esta call upon her attached bloodline as she almost slipped into oblivion. Esta accepted her role as one of the Hands of Silthar. The nature of the Hands of Silthar was similar but different from that of those that bore the blessing of the Lord of Blood. The Hands of Silthar could absorb portions of their bloodline's sustenance to sustain significant portions of damage. Yet at the cost of their Sanghilis to overtake their mind. A constant threat.

She beat it back and devoured the corrupted essence with all the fury of a dying star. She blinked and tried to reach out to Vedus, but his mind was clouded in a sea of shadows. Something fought back against her. Pain rose in her mind as she reeled back and returned to her vision.

Lowering her hand, she brushed fingers atop the collar of her armour. As it dragged across the cold metal, a clasp formed. This was an ancient spell she pulled from the armour, a bygone era when the Gods walked the surface of Calisine. A silver clasp manifested underneath her fingers with a vampiric bat emblazoned on the surface. She felt the ancient energy come to life, as behind her, what looked to be made out of sinew and blood, it writhed with faces and muted cries of pain. The Mantle of Silthar was the spell's name. Shaving a piece of the cloak that brimmed with the power of Silthar could spawn a creature from the realm of blood.

Waving her hand in the air, her eyes blazed with power as she moved through air and reality and blinked. She stood atop the temple of Alrizhod, looking upon the vampires that took back their place as rulers of the night.

Scanning the streets, she connected eyes with Esta and raised her hand, appearing as though she clutched the moon and commanded Tantibrus to find weapons and armour and slay the enemies of the Children of Silthar.

They obeyed, as they spread out and rushed to the armoury, she reached out and connected herself to the minds of all the freed vampires. Still perturbed by the resistance of Vedus, the night would be theirs once more.

Chapter Twenty-Two: The City Awakens

Hours passed, and blood and steel exchanged within lifelong moments. At last, the rebellion of the Children of Silthar had begun. Their shackles were torn and given freedom, turning upon their lizard masters. Vedus freed as many as possible; the total number that joined Esta and Sana's rebellion grew beyond his comprehension. He stopped counting the number he saved after one-hundred and eighty-seven. They had a sizable resistance force on their hands, well-outfitted and ready to retake the night.

Vedus wandered the streets for a time, freeing every possible vampire he laid eyes on. Each time he freed them, he felt something within him grow. This crusade of blood did not have to involve him. He felt a stranger to their cause as the streets were stained red.

Sheathing his sword, as he wandered one of the ruined wards of the city, the obsidian black skeletons of buildings rose to the sky, begging to return. He could feel the history of the town as he walked the ruined paths. Black dust and long-forgotten bone dust kicked up with each step. The rain had stopped, leaving clouded skies as the night slowly settled and gave life to morning.

As he walked through the graveyard of ancient buildings, he heard Vastra as she asked, *"Why do you help them?"*

It was a simple question, one that he struggled to find the answer to. "... They need me."

Vastra stepped from the shadows as though she had remained there all this time. She wore a dress of stars, with those collapsing suns that laid eyes upon him as she repeated aloud, "Use you is more like it."

"What?" Vedus shrugged and faced Vastra; she seemed perturbed by something.

Vastra was unamused, crossing her arms and gesturing to his wrist, "I hoped you were stronger to resist my mother's magic. Do not think yourself foolish. Most mortals are reduced to a grovelling mess when they lay eyes upon her."

"I felt inclined to accept her gifts. She brought me back to life."

She rolled her eyes as she said, "Do you not remember that she is the Goddess of temptations and deceit? She brought you back to life because she wanted something. Something that only you can give her."

"What is it?"

"I don't know," Vastra shrugged, keeping themselves in a ruined one-room house, "I was hoping you would tell me."

Vedus felt his blood boil as he wandered the collapsed walls of the house they found themselves in. Half of the building was missing, with a huge gaping hole in the top left side of the building. A shattered bench was all the furnishings of the house, a slave's quarters, he assumed. They had passed by a larger construct, more intact, which he presumed owned the slave's quarters.

So many people needed him, and for what? He knew nothing. Nothing important should garner the attention of vampires and the Goddess of Shadows. With how many powerful beings needed an audience with him, he would have assumed that his need was obvious.

She drew in closer, gathering his attention to her once more as she said, "But we cannot know if you succumb to my mother's will. Your true self will be locked away, and you will be little more than a husk, ready to please my mother's whims."

Vedus studied her. She seemed to harbour no ill will. His time in the court of Eternium taught him to read people's bodies for their true intentions. She showed no visible signs of wishing to harm him in any way, physical or non-physical. But perhaps the lingering deathly fear told him not to trust her. He was not about to trust anyone entirely after one of his father's most trusted advisors murdered him.

He asked, "Why do you want to help me? How do I know that your intentions are true?"

Vastra smiled, pleased with the fact that he questioned everything. She seemed to be expecting that answer. "I choose not to live in my mother's large shadow. I refuse to follow in her footsteps. I am helping you because I have had to bear witness to countless souls stripped of everything that makes them who they are until only a shell of themselves remains, no loyalty, no independence, just blind pleasure and desire to serve my mother."

Vastra almost whispered as she continued, "If I harboured any ill will towards you, then why would I give you the location of armour to help suppress the whispers of the shadows?"

Vedus countered, "Perhaps you want to get me into a false sense of security."

Vastra furrowed her brow for a few moments and said, "With paranoia like that, I would think that you would have split off from Esta and Sana by now."

"How do you know about them?"

"You mortals are terribly easy to track, especially ones that recently died and have no idea the magic held within him."

"I don't need to fathom what power resides within. I want to be left alone."

She studied him for a moment, looking past his flesh and boring into his soul. What was left of it anyway. He was sure that she saw something that he did not. Gods and their children were always ones for revealing minute details about one's soul that they knew nothing about.

Her sun-like eyes met him once more. "Do you think you can return from the dead without consequences?"

"I am not some rare commodity to be traded off." He said defensively, stepping back against ancient dust, crunching under the weight of his heels. The clouds parted for a moment, and the day's greyscale faded with the sun's bleeding rays. He relished the moment until he felt the dull fog return. He wondered what secrets lay within the ruined walls of the house he stood upon.

She seemed conceded by this point and said, "You choose your path, Vedus. If you wish to live a life of a spectre and never know the answers you need, then who am I to stop you."

Before disappearing into the shadows, she said, "I am not your enemy. I want to help, from one wayward soul to another."

She was gone; replacing her was Sana as she stalked closer with her new retinue. They had outfitted themselves well. Bound in aged iron plates, they followed closely behind her. They were all unfamiliar with such weight. For some, it was the first time they took up a sword.

Something changed about her. She had an aura of power that rolled off of her. She wore form-fitted black steel plate armour. It appeared light upon her and sacrificed none of her mobility. Rather than appear as though she was wearing armour, it was shaped to look more like chitinous armour similar to a scorpion's.

He went back to the camp and felt the shadows talk into his mind, he lifted his hand with the gift given to him by the Queen of Shadows, and his four servants peeled from the shadowed walls. Their garb did not change.

Vallia leaned in close and whispered, "Are you ready?"

He shook his head as he felt his mind rend with whispering darkness and replied, "But she is a vampire; she can hear me coming."

Salaia responded, "You have no heartbeat, and you step with the shadows now. She will be caught totally unaware."

He felt his mind carve away all thought as he looked into her eyes. Deep within them, he saw the lust for him to succeed. They begged and pleaded with him to carry out this task, and he felt unwilling to avoid it or say no.

As he nodded, they disappeared, and all whispered to him, "Then go carry out the Queen's will. We have faith in you, prince."

He stalked over to where they were staying. He could not help but feel like he did not belong. The hunger in their eyes was insatiable. They craved more than blood, and vengeance raged like a storm within them.

He found Esta, who was doffing her armour near the armoury and said, "Where's Sana? I want to speak with her."

Esta removed her breastplate and cloak and said, "She's at the bathhouse. Apparently, Ilthauns like to stay clean."

Vedas nodded and turned to leave when she said, "Are you okay, Vedus? You're not acting like yourself."

"I'm fine. I just need to talk to Sana."

Esta took off her belt and said, "Look, I know that you're going through a lot, and I know that you don't share the same feelings as all of us."

"How do you know that?"

She replied with a smile. "Call it a soldier's intuition. I know when someone is not fit for a cause they either don't understand or don't want to be a part of."

Leaning against the table, her eyes narrowed and grew more serious. "And I know when a soldier is given orders that they didn't want to hear."

Vedus grit his teeth. "I know what I'm doing."

Unmoving, Esta questioned. "Do you? Sana told me about your incident when you were practising "drills." It seems to me that your hold is slipping."

Vedus turned to leave and said before he crossed the threshold, "Don't pretend you care. You'll use me for your ends and then cast me aside. I'm just a corpse, anyway. I wouldn't expect you to care."

It felt as though no time had passed when he trudged through the streets of Alrizhod. Whatever happened, geometry did not alter his perception of reality anymore. Vedus suspected it was due to Sana gaining control of their newest recruits. Her will was strong. He could feel it.

He tensed his arm, looked at the silvered bracelet, and continued on his path.

The bathhouse was on the far side of the city, near where the Skithik invaded. The streets were being cleaned of the bodies and the blood.

The steam from the bathhouse could be felt even before he stepped past the threshold.

He unsheathed his sword and stalked down the entrance and to the pools beyond. The room opened wide and could comfortably hold forty or more people. Vedus suspected this was kept for the former slaves of the Ilthauns. Their moment of peace before they continued their work.

She stood amidst the steam, her pale skin glowing from the candlelight. Vedus always knew there was some truth that elves held beauty in high regard. Vedus almost felt entranced by her form. Sana was one of the most beautiful women he had ever seen. Her long silvery locks looked as though they were captured rays of moonlight.

Vedus carefully stepped forward; she was unaware. The shadows bade him step forward. Sword poised and ready to strike. Even as he stepped into the waist-high water, there was no sound. He did not disturb the waters with his undead form. It was as if the shadows guided him.

Combing her hands through her hair, she leaned down cupped water into her hands, letting the water gently rain down her face.

He stopped a metre away from her, his sword raised and inches away from piercing her back.

The shadows grew louder and guided his hand.

His hand trembled as he stood ready to strike.

"And what are you hoping to accomplish?"

His breath stopped, his heart sank into his stomach.

She slowly turned and faced him. Before she could say another word, guided by shadows, he thrust his sword deep into her chest. Blood leaking from her chest, she looked down and into his eyes. Shocked, his lip quivered. He had known her for so many days, and she trusted him to aid her and Esta in their task, and this was his repayment?

He wrenched his sword from her chest, and his breath began to increase as her form limply fell to the ground steadily.

As soon as she hit the water, her form evaporated into red and black wisps of energy.

"I had faith in you, Prince Vedus."

He turned and saw Sana drying her hair at the entrance to the pools.

Shocked, he found no words and kept his sword at the ready.

Sana smiled half-heartedly and said, "You think me a fool to be unguarded in a bathhouse? Not to mention, I heard you unsheathe your sword at the entrance though I did not expect to see you."

Pulling over a linen robe, she folded her arms expectantly. "I take it you have given in to the Queen's demands?"

His sword arm shook as he replied. "It's the only way to make it stop."

She shrugged her shoulders. "Who am I to stand in the way of a God? It's quite amusing that the affairs of the Queen of Shadows are involved here. Only fitting since it was your Queen that made Silthar what he is now."

His voice trembled as he said, averting his gaze. "You… you still need me."

"You're right. I would open your neck right now if I didn't. But I have a distinct feeling that your patron will punish you enough for your failure."

She was a metre away from him, guiding his sword away with her fingers as she lifted his chin to look her in the eyes. "So, we are going to forget that this happened. We will carry out our task to kill the leadership of the Skithik—"

Sana thrust her hand against his throat and lifted him off the ground. His sword clattered to the bottom of the pool, clutching her hand as he gasped for air. Her firm grip threatened to crush his windpipe.

She pulled him close and extended her fangs. "But as soon as we are done, I will tear off your head and keep your soul alive long enough to make you watch as I drain every last drop of blood from your body."

She released him and walked out of the bathhouse as he clutched his neck. Coughing into the water, he shook as he now had no plan for what to do. He closed his eyes as he felt hands rest upon him, and he heard Vallia's voice in his ear as she said, "The Queen will not be happy."

Chapter Twenty-Three: Blood Against Blood

Esta

For days they established and solidified their rebellion. They knew it would not be an easy task to mount a proper revolt against the Skithik. Sana left Esta in charge of training them how to fight. It was not perfect, they still had room to improve, but they could last in a fight.

The following month they spent gathering intel on their lizard foes. Sana sent out Tantibrus, naming them the Tantibrus Legion and would be their agents of subterfuge. When they returned, they proved invaluable to their cause and discovered a weak point they could use to infiltrate their city.

They had a few moments to face their reptilian foes, sending out auxiliary forces to deal with the growing rebellion. The last thing the Skithik needed was another Blood Crusade to begin. They would never recover from the division. They represented all of the worst traits of vampirism. They were bloodlust incarnate. And it sickened Esta to a degree. She never thought she would be sickened by another purely because of their malformed viewpoint. Two months later, they were still establishing their operations. Fortifications began before that first month ended. However, the fortifications could not be completed.

Esta entered the murky waters, fit and prepared for battle. She took with her Korugul and Gethin, the most prized members of her bloodline. Getting to know those whom she claimed, she began to feel part of something. She buried her insecurities and could feel herself begin to beat back those self-destructive thoughts she knew all too well. She could breathe easily, knowing she was somewhat comfortable with herself.

Her mission was twofold: Rescue any remaining vampiric slaves and bring back as much stone as possible. She brought with her a band of twelve animated corpses to pull the stones back to Alrizhod. Not since six months ago did she walk with so much confidence. Their frames were large; Esta presumed them to be part of the giant family somewhere between a goliath and an ettin. The necromancer that commanded them wore dark robes and runes of necrotic protection etched and scratched onto the obsidian surface. He was a Sanguinaire like Sana, and his name was Belanor. The first necromancer of her bloodline. Sana was quick to teach those capable of learning magic. To a certain degree, all vampires were capable of using magic. Esta herself knew a handful of spells, but her reserves were not quite as large as the necromancer's and certainly not even close in size to Sana's reserves. She bled magic from every pore.

Hours passed as they trudged through muck and then through the sand. Nothing broke their stride. They crested a dune that rose high. After reaching the top, she raised her hand for the rest of them to stop. Belanor motioned for the behemoths to cease. They moaned as they came to a stop. Belanor, Korugul, and Gethin joined Esta at the top and crouched along with her as she began to look at the city. It had not changed since she last laid eyes upon it, other than the fact that she now looked at it with more ire now that she was free. Esta thought back to shouldering stones out of the mines.

"What's the plan?" asked Korugul.

Esta studied Ardarian, her eyes dancing over the simplistic port town. She drew her eyes over to the mine and then back to the city proper. She slowly developed a plan and mused, "We will split into two groups. Gethin and Belanor, you two will take ten of the behemoths to the mine and secure it, kill any Skithik that try to stop you. Korugul and I will take two of the behemoths and rescue any vampires in the city. It is night, and a good portion of them might still be working in the mine, but there are ships docked, leaving me to believe that a new wave of vampire recruits is in the city somewhere. In three hours, we will meet back at the mine entrance."

They all nodded. Esta gathered the attention of Belanor and asked, "You know the sanctification spell, correct?"

She referred to a more effective spell that Sana taught all necromancers when they received their training. It was a simple divine spell that would summon fire to the scarabs embedded in their necks.

Belanor nodded, "Yes, I remember the spell."

"Good." Esta motioned for Korugul, and under her breath, she commanded two of the behemoths to follow her. The black language of Silandor, the language of necromancy, was not a strong suit of Esta. She knew a few of the commands for controlling the undead, but she did not know many phrases. She looked to Korugul as he hefted a greataxe, the orcish blood that flowed through his veins eager to carry its weight. Neither of them felt awkward speaking with one another, considering her history standing against Kodlan Khane and his invading army. Still, she knew that half-orcs were not considered to be welcomed with kindness to their pureblooded brethren. Something they both could relate to.

He had scars and markings along his arms. The runic language of orcs and elves often intertwined, orcish being a dialect of the elvish runic language. Rather than amplifying arcane forces, orcish runes were more suppressive and permanent when marked unto a mortal's flesh. He was a Null, a mortal devoid of magic with no possible way to gain a reservoir of magic. Too many hideous markings ran the length of his arms and back.

They were an insecurity to him. She knew this by the way he would hide them. There was always pain behind his eyes when he looked at them. Esta never pressed the issue. That was for him to reveal when the time was right.

At the bottom of the dune, Esta unsheathed Blacksun, humming with a deep necrotic tune as it glided through the air.

****

They reached the edge of the city, the wooden walls hiding their movements well, clinging to the shadows of the walls. The plan was to secure the docks first and gather any vampires that way. Another reason for taking Ardarian was to secure a path to the mainland once the Skithik were decimated.

The wind was foul with the stench of corruption and pain, dancing over their still forms as they stalked through the shadows of the wooden wall. She grew accustomed to her new armour, scalemail with a breastplate and shoulder guards. A black waist cape fluttered in the silent breeze. A long cloth scarf draped over her shoulders and wrapped loosely around her neck joined the dance of the wind. The ceramic bone knives she gained from her recent kill rested comfortably on her belt.

Korugul boasted heavier steel plate armour with the same insectoid look that most had. His scarf was long and did well to cover his arms. Wrapped around his mouth as well. A single-shoulder guard stood upon his left shoulder. It glinted in the waning moonlight.

She drew her attention to the wall as they listened, their breaths stopping as they heard the Skithik patrolling the top of the walls, their scraping talons loud against the wooden floors beneath them. They passed them by without so much as a glance.

Their breaths returned as she ordered the behemoths to hoist them up. Vaulting over the parapets of the wall, they slinked back into the shadows, looking left and then right. The sturdy wooden walls, reinforced by iron clamps, stretched the length of the port city. The buildings within boasted the same savage structure to them. It was a city of necessity, their fortifications were decent, but they were nothing sophisticated. Skithiks were not ones to be proud of their architecture. They built what they needed and nothing more.

With her off-hand, she gestured in the air, and black and red magic danced over the form of her hand. Reaching through the darkness, she commanded the behemoths to find the main gate and wait for them.

Ceasing the spell, she motioned for Korugul to follow her. She counted them lucky that Korugul's armour was not noisy. She was no smith, but she knew the material of the plate armour they found in Alrizhod was Eldarian, a metal often used by the Ilthauns. Lightweight, sturdy, and easy to manipulate. With the armour protection, Sana and their newly trained spell casters infused the armour with some magical wards. They were nothing substantial, but they could last through a few battles without denting too heavily.

They skirted along the walls doing well to find the main gate. When they came upon the roofed structure, they stopped and moved to either side of the door.

Peeking through the shadows, she saw a singular large Skithik leaning against a pillar, snoozing gently. Esta motioned to Korugul to stay put. After another spell, her form shifted into a dark mist. With quickened steps, she slithered through the room and approached the sleeping Skithik guard. Reforming from the shadows, she plunged her blade deep through its chest, her other hand clamping its maw shut as it struggled to shout.

Esta whistled briefly and quietly as she could, and Korugul entered the room. Setting down his axe, he approached one side of the crank and whispered, "There are two of them coming this way, making their rounds."

"We'll have to be quick then." She said, setting down the dead Skithik and sheathing her blade.

Grabbing the other side of the crank, they began the slow process of opening the gate in unison. The weight of the chains, coupled with the weight of the thick wooden gate doors, made the action considerably cumbersome. They both strained with all their might as they heard the gate slowly open.

They went as fast as they could, rushing to try and open the gate. As it was about halfway open, they strained against it as it would not move anymore. It was jammed. Reaching out, she willed the door to the gatehouse to shut. As it slammed closed, she rushed over to keep it shut and watched as sweat dripped from Korugul's brow. Straining as he forced the gate to unjam.

She reached out to the behemoths and ordered them to pry the gate the rest of the way open for them. They did as they were commanded. As one, Korugul and they struggled to unjam the gate. Esta could feel the Skithik approaching; they were steps away, her blood freezing at the fear that they would be caught.

The chains whined as they continued their path to open the gate.

She held the door closed as Korugul rushed to prop up the dead Skithik. When he finished, he darted for the adjoining doorway on the other side of the gatehouse. She disappeared into a formless ethereal mist as he left and rushed over to the dead Skithik, preparing to respond

As they opened the door to the gatehouse, she greeted them with a nod of the head. They then asked him something and gestured towards the gate chains. She puppeteered him to shrug and watched as one of them grew agitated and left. The second stood for a moment, narrowing his eyes, and promptly left.

Letting the body slump forward and fall back to the ground, she left on the far side exit and joined Korugul with his axe ready.

They exchanged no words as they continued towards the docks.

***

Rushing through the empty streets, they quietly dashed towards the docks. She knew the general direction; she was ordered to send the stone into Ardarian several times. How different her life had changed over the course of the last few months. From slave to runaway to Lord-Sire. She almost did not believe it. It all happened so fast.

The shadows of the buildings did well to hide their movements. If she recalled correctly, the nightly patrols were quite the tired bunch.

They found their way to the docks and kept to the shadows as they searched the portside ships for any slaves. They searched, finding only a handful left. This led them to believe they had already been sorted and prepared for their reconditioning.

Knowing where they were being held, they found them. The Skithik had received three hundred new slaves to recondition and use. Many of them were from Aebolon, from their postured and proud stances. What seemed even odder was that most wore the brand of the Shepherds of Revendor, the knight-protectors of the mages and the realms.

She noted this and counted her blessings that they had experienced soldiers in their midst. They were found out when they finished untying them and removing their scarabs.

It did not take them long to retake the city; in the blink of an eye, control had swiftly found its way into their camp. And for one gleaming moment, Esta could see their victory at hand.

Chapter Twenty-Four: Council of Blood

Ardarian was taken with little more than a hush in the night. Securing stone and more soldiers for their rebellion, they could see the end goal of plunging the Skithik into a rebellion that they would not see coming. They had to deal with some of the patrols of the Skithik but never full-blown companies of warriors. They had an army at their disposal and had yet to use it. This concerned Sana greatly and picked at her still. Many of the patrols they captured and used as cattle to feed.

They fashioned their rebellious flags from their skin and reinforced their steel with their marrow, any chance they could get to insult the Skithik they took.

Esta waved a hand in front of Sana, pulling her from her stupor, and said, "Sana? Are you still with us?"

Sana waved a hand, "Yes, I'm fine. You were talking about the siege?"

Esta gestured back to the war table, a map of Urstron splayed out after a scouting mission a few months back. The war council consisted of the Bloodlords: Esta being one of them, another being Alaric from the former Shepherds of Revendor, who asked to speak with her once the council was adjourned. Avina, who led the necromancers and proved to be a valuable asset and practitioner of magic, and Bloodlord Zelphar Ralocan—one of the Dreadnoughts of the Sanguinaire. Of course, the last of the council was Prince Vedus Ostrogoth, whom she kept a close eye on. The last she needed was for him to become a turncoat because of the power he was unworthy to wield.

Esta's voice was loud as she said, "We will send a decoy contingent with the heads and banners we made to get the attention of the Skithik. While they are charging out, another contingent will descend from the mountains. This group will fight and secure the gates, opening them for the returning contingent and the main body of our forces."

The Tantibrus Legion was ordered to remain behind and protect the city with what soldiers they had left. Altogether they had three thousand vampires and two thousand zombies and skeletons.

Alaric crossed his arms and said in a gruff and deep voice, "I understand that we have nothing in terms of siege weaponry, but no skeleton or zombie of ours could withstand the blizzards of those mountains."

Avina spoke and said, "We do not have the spells or materials to make them resistant to the elements; they could last if they remained in the desert."

Esta shrugged and said, "Then let them be the decoy group, and we can descend from the mountains."

Zelphar shook his head, "They have the blood of a dead God to use at their disposal. They will surely see all of this coming."

Sana spoke, silencing the murmurs between the Bloodlords, and said, "I took careful measurements to mask our movements from the prying eyes of the blood-scryers of the Skithik."

Zelphar nodded and returned his gaze to the map.

Vedus, who remained quiet until this point, leaned against the table and said, "Why not from within?"

Sana notched an eyebrow, and Alaric asked her question, "What do you mean?"

Vedus shrugged, "What if we turned ourselves in and sprang our trap that way? Secure the gate and signal the main body of our forces to charge through and take the city."

Zelphar said, "That is assuming that they don't kill us immediately on sight."

Avina shook her head, "They are tribal and savage. Their only response to betrayal is bloodshed."

Vedus defiantly stood his ground and said, "And they are still immensely ceremonial. They understand the surrender of one tribe to another. Entertain the thought of requesting parlay with them to discuss a joining of forces while they are unsuspecting of our whereabouts. We kill their leadership, secure the gate, and secure control of Urstron."

Silence fell upon the war council, their eyes heavy and their minds racing to find the perfect plan for them to follow to ensure a quick and decisive victory. She could feel the weight of leadership upon their shoulders, fear creeping at the edges of their minds, a distant shadow but a present one that they would be foolish to ignore. There was always a chance of failure, but they would live free before falling into the midst of capture again. Flashing images of her endured cruelty caused her to blink and sit up.

She shook her head to Vedus, "It is too risky, Vedus. I will not risk being captured again and enduring more torture just for a victory. Many of my people already suffer from the trauma of being a slave to the Skithik; I would not ask them to go through it again."

Vedus's expression darkened, and he said, "Your people know what to expect; I'm sure they would—"

"I could not bear the thought of them enduring more pain than they already have."

"So you throw yourselves at them? And fall from the peaks to catch them off guard? All this, and they have very little training in warfare. I'm sorry, but what is being suggested is essentially throwing them right to the mouths of wolves."

Sana stood up and set her jaw and shoulders fiercely, "You are no citizen of mine. If you wish to continue your plan, then do so yourself. I will not sacrifice the dignity of my people just for victory. They seemed to take a liking to you, give you special treatment while they had you in their chains. You can be all the distraction we need."

Vedus cracked a brief smile and said, "So be it."

He let himself out, and they finished securing their plans for the invasion. She questioned her harshness towards Vedus, but ultimately it came down to the simple fact of they were not his citizens to command. They were hers. And she would not let such cruelty into their damaged minds anymore. She could feel their fears, their nightmares of pain and misery. No more.

As they were getting ready to part ways, Alaric pulled her aside and said, "What was it you wanted to tell me?"

He clenched his jaw for a moment and said in a low voice, "Ketos has fallen. After the death of King Valamer Ostrogoth, the realms were plunged into war. The elves were the first to fall under the blades of the new Emperor,

Vorkalth. The Dwarves were next to fall. He split the Shepherds of Revendor and caused a civil war in my order."

Sana's worry grew with each word he spoke, he paused as he remembered the pain of fighting his brothers and sisters of the order, "Who stood against him?"

He choked back and said, regaining his composure, "The Wizards were the only ones able to put them in a stalemate. Though I don't know how much longer they can hold against them, Vorkalth has found a way to nullify magic completely. And last I heard, they were setting their sights on destroying Weylines."

Sana absorbed this information and, deeply disturbed, said, "Then, once we are done here, we will send whatever aid we can to them."

"They're all dead. The elves of Sarthalas. They were brought to extinction."

Biting her lip, she absorbed that fact and said, "Then we will send all our troops to aid the last defenders of the Eternium."

She could see and feel despair towards this subject. He was not hopeful of her optimism. Neither was she; it was a lot for her to take in. She did her best but buried her feelings for another time. She calmly breathed out and exuded leadership and courage as she was taught. A war on two fronts would overextend them. She would need to reach out to her bloodline on Nostra if they were to succeed in this coming war.

She nodded and said to Alaric, "Thank you for informing me of this information. Get some rest. We have much work to do."

He bowed, and as he turned to leave, she watched the door that Vedus had left a few moments ago. She prayed to Silthar that he would live to see this end. He was their only chance at killing the leadership of the Skithik. She just prayed they did not know that.

Chapter Twenty-Five: Potency

Esta

Esta coughed as dust burst in front of her, waving her hand to expel the gathering particles. Within the crate, she saw a pile of belongings that once belonged to some of her bloodline. Their thoughts became nothing more than distant whispers as she finally had a moment to think. Their constant needs beckoned her action. Her headache finally subsided after days of brokering her attention between her sires.

Amongst the munitions and satchels, she did find a few weapons, nothing more than a few shortswords or daggers. Very few of her sires proved to have any proper skill with a weapon. Esta's tired muscles from leading her sires in drills did well to remind her as such.

Lifting a shield from the clutter, her left arm flared in a brief pain. A stabbing pain within her joint. Setting it down, she rubbed the disturbed area to alleviate the pain. Recent days and constant training had led to her previous wound reminding her of the fateful day she lost a limb. The scar was nearly invisible, but the memory of the pain remained.

Before, she had the comfort of poetry and a daily journal to gather her thoughts and remind her of her humanity. However, without the need for sleep or rest of any kind, she had no such comfort. The words she wrote felt like distant ghosts that bore no meaning—empty words to fill a page. There was very little that could distract her from her mission, let alone her duties leading a bloodline.

The distant rays of the moon peeked through the windows of the storehouse. It's gelid rays washed over the ground and nipped her skin. Foregoing her breastplate, her only armour worn was her sabatons and bracers. A black tunic and trousers wrapped around her were her only shield against the numb air.

Making a mental note of the total amount of weapons and munitions within, she marched over to a small desk by the large doors leading to the streets of Ardarian. Quickly jotting down the total, she continued her task, grabbing the crate and stacking it amongst the other seventy-six near the doors. From her estimate, they would need to forge very few new weapons and armour. The Song of War rages on, as they say.

One shelving unit had been nearly picked clean. Pushing two crates aside, she saw a long wooden crate. Slender and nearly as tall as her. This struck her as odd. Thus far, the other crates were of standard size. If these belonged to one of her bloodline, she assumed they were once a spearman or a fisherman.

With the barest flinch, the nailed crate surrendered to her strength and nearly splintered. Within, however, caused her to pause. These were her belongings.

Each piece of armour, leather, rucksack, shield, spear, and sword. It was all there. She thought for sure that due to how long she was imprisoned that her belongings would have been lost or melted down.

Her hands shook as she rested a hand on her former breastplate. She brushed it, the tarnished metal brazing her flesh. Drawing her hand away revealed the misshapen insignia of the Eternium she once served. An eagle with six wings, each wing representing the six nations that united to keep Ketos safe from invaders. Her mind swirled with the memories of joining the infantry of the Eternium only a few years before the start of the Olkhan Invasion. The sprawling fields of the White Vale, the emerald green trees of Sarthalas, and the snowy caps of Arnthor became her home when her family abandoned her, leaving her to the elements with little care. It felt like a lifetime ago.

Her hand shook, and her eyes bleary from mustering tears, lip quivering from what she thought were lost memories. She was stronger back then. She could face down the gathering lines of orcs without fear. Now she could not think of fighting without letting the memory of her nearly fatal wound come to mind.

A voice broke the silence. "Why are you weeping?"

On instinct, she answered, without properly hearing whose voice it was, thinking it to be one of her sires. "Because I can't… I can't carry on like this."

"As you are or what you were?"

Upon hearing those words, she wiped her tears and turned to confirm her fears. There, standing in the light of the moon, was her brother, Ezran Desidarius. His long black hair was tied back, revealing a chiselled stubbly jaw and piercing golden eyes. He wore scalemail, faceted and polished with excellent care. A long green cloak drifted slightly in the night breeze wafted from an open window. Four swords sheathed at both his sides and two on his back. He did not bear an expression of mute stoicism that she usually saw. She saw pity in his eyes.

Hate overtook her sadness as her lip quivered. "You wouldn't understand, Ezran… you're not even real."

He answered, "I'm a manifestation of how you see him. I'm as close to real without him being here."

"Am I mad? Have I lost my sanity just like Vedus?" She said as she shook her head, closing the top of the crate.

Slightly shaking his head, he replied. "Far from it, I'm you. I'm your Sangilis made into physical form. You saw me before when–"

"Don't."

"How much longer can you push away everything? You refuse to embrace what you are fully. You tolerate it to have your gifts, but you refuse to embrace it for what it is."

Throwing the crate to the shelf, she burst to her feet and faced her twin. "I'm tired of all of it! I'm unravelling! I can't move on, but I can't step backward! I want it all to end, but I can't be the hand that delivers the final blow. And you are *not* the one to tell me what I am and am not. That's–"

"Your responsibility?"

"I hate you…." Clenching her hands and shaking her head, hoping to open her eyes and see no one there.

"No, you don't."

A storm festered within her. A tempest of rage and jealousy washed over her in waves. She could feel her Sangilis and Blacksun vying for control, both gnawing at her wounded psyche. She wondered if the anger belonged to her or if Blacksun and her Sangilis brought forth their own interpretation of how she should react. Bracing her hand against one of the supports for the shelf, she squeezed and heard the wood begin to splinter and crack under her supernatural strength.

Breathing deeply, she remembered Sana's words and eased out, "Was there any hope? For us both, after what we did?"

Stepping closer, he replied, "We both survived, didn't we?"

Esta chortled, "I hardly endured."

Ezran shook his head. "You're too harsh on yourself. The pedestal you have for your brother is nearly insurmountable."

"How am I supposed to live up to what he can do? I'm no different than how everyone else sees him. They'd sooner instil their faith in him rather than the Gods. He's never disappointed. He's never faltered. They clamber to hold him to the same standards as the Heroes of Calisine. And they see me, his twin, to uphold the same standard. I can't... I *can't!*"

The wood broke under her grip, the nearly empty shelf almost collapsing due to fallen support. They craved more, Blacksun and her Sangilis. They ushered a flood of visions into her mind that bore nothing but pain and misery. For the briefest of moments, she invited it.

Ezran shrugged. "So what will you do? Kill him?"

Her veins rushed with adrenaline as she replied with a cruel smile. "They'd certainly change their mind about me. I'd be lying if I said that I never had the thought."

"I'm not your enemy. He's not your enemy."

Resting her hand calmly on the shelf, she drummed her fingers against the soft wood. "Arrogance is potent. Though you never had to hear that, did you? Rage is a corrosive weapon. You never had to hear that, either. You filled everyone with so much pride that you avoided the hard lessons. I had to crawl so you could run. While I drew the ire of our family, you became their pristine avatar. I bore witness to their silent cruelty. You were cradled. You were spared from their abuse. You aren't me, and I'm not you, but I know *you* felt the same."

Cocking his head to the side, garnering that smug stoic look, he said, "What do you want?"

In a blink, she rushed over to Ezran and gripped his neck, pressing him against the adjacent shelf, nearly knocking it over. With murderous intent in her eyes, she licked her lips, revealing extended canines. "*We* want nothing more than to see every last drop of blood drain from your sorry corpse."

He did not falter, not even a quiver of fear. But he did squirm uncomfortably underneath her grip despite the force that threatened to crush his windpipe.

Not faltering, she said, "You have lorded over me for far too long. I can't let you stand in my way again. I'll paint the walls with your blood...."

"Esta."

"... I've finally got the clarity I need! I can't move forward without killing you first...."

"Esta."

"... Perhaps I'll be even stronger from your pristine blood. I'll fill *rivers* with it."

"Esta, please!"

"What!" Esta slammed her eyes shut and rendered control back over to herself. She felt their essences rip as she tore them away, peeling their sinking claws of control from her damaged mind, casting them back into the dark oblivion that once harboured her soul. Blacksun and her Sangilis screamed as they fell into the black.

Opening her eyes slowly, she choked on her words. In her grip was Sana, her eyes pleading.

Esta started to shake, the adrenaline washing away. "Sana?... By the Pantheon... I'm sorry... I'm sorry...."

Releasing her hand from Sana's throat, Esta gripped both sides of her head as the headache she suppressed returned. It wrapped its iron-like grip around the width of her head and tightened. Throbbing, she felt Blacksun and her Sangilis fester once more. She muttered, "I can't do this… I can't do this anymore… I can't do this!–"

Sana pressed her hands against Sana's cheeks. "Esta, look at me."

Looking into twin scarlet suns, Esta squinted her eyes and felt a soothing calm wash over her mind. Whether it was from some psychic magic or just from looking into the eyes of someone familiar, she did not know. However, she could not help but feel calmed by them. Once they brought her ire, now they soothed her troubled mind.

In one singular moment, she felt herself regain control and rested her head against Sana's shoulder and braced her in for a hug. Her fingers dug into Sana's back, pleading. "Thank you…."

Sana returned the hug. "I'm always right here."

Breathing in for one moment longer, Esta stepped away. "How did you know? When did you come in?"

Sana dusted herself off. She wore a long evening dress of light grey. "I heard you shouting, and I feared I was too late to help you. I stepped in at the back half of the… *conversation*. It was me that said you're too harsh on yourself."

Nodding, a single tear ran down Esta's cheek. "You're not wrong…."

Folding her hands together, Sana nodded towards the doors and said, "Follow me."

Chapter Twenty-Six: The Hands of Blood

With the pallid light of the moon to guide them, Esta followed Sana as they wandered the streets of Ardarian. It silently bustled with the muted steps of the freed Sanguinaire. There was a time when Esta thought that to be a term for the elven vampires, but any that follow the path of Silthar are granted the right to be called Sanguinaire. She was worthy of an afterlife. She had to do nothing to prove herself to gain. What little comfort it did bring paled in comparison to the festering within.

They walked until they left the dusted walls and unto the dunes. They climbed up and up, the sand sparkling in the light of the moon. Her muscles finally stopped shaking, not from exhaustion but from the disquieted moment only a few minutes ago. Her head felt heavy, scarred from the control she willingly gave to Blacksun and her Sangilis. She did not hear her bloodline whisper to her. Their incessant prayers felt like distant memories.

They stopped at the top of the tallest dune, Sana turning to face Esta. The half-elf couldn't help but look away. Before, she threatened her life for a selfish reason, now, she had no excuse.

Sana said, "You don't need to feel sorry for what happened."

Esta clenched her sore fist and gritted her teeth. "It's easy for you to say that you're not the one that almost killed someone without reason. Each life I take has to serve a purpose. Each life lost is meant to bring me closer to–"

"Your death?" Sana folded her hands and shook her head. "For someone with so much hate for their family, you certainly do well to carry their traditions. The good and the bad."

Esta instinctively sat down. The sand soothed her and reminded her of a life that did not feel real. "It's all that I've known… I don't know anything else."

Sana sat next to her, crossing her legs. "You've spent decades away from them, living amongst folk of all walks of life. None of them spoke to you after what your family did to you?"

Digging her finger in the sand, Esta gave a half-hearted chuckle. "Despite all the pain I endured, I still can't separate myself from them."

Sana's face drained for a moment as she replied, "That's how the cycle repeats, dearest Esta."

Esta grabbed a fistful of sand. As each grain drifted back down, every sorrow resurfaced. Every lashing, every talking to, every moment of control. She buried them in hopes that they could be forgotten, hoping to learn from them. Yet here she was, unable to retain control of her anger. All those years of training to control it were brought down in a matter of seconds. To rebuild would mean starting from the beginning, and Esta had no clue where to begin building her foundation.

Sana looked up. "We begin life thinking the stars belong to us. Our home was once amongst them, at Iara's side. If such things were true, why were we born so far away from them?"

Esta narrowed her brow. "Are you quoting Delsaran?"

Sana nodded. "Indeed. The first elven scholar to challenge the traditions of the elves. He theorised that rather than leaving the home of the elves at Iara's side to find her lost throne, we were cast out, and that is why we were claimed by Beros the Eternal Conquest. He sought the truth behind the long ancient traditions, he challenged every method of thought that made the elves what they are. Despite how he was raised, despite all of the ridicule he faced."

Esta shook her head. "Why?"

Sana shrugged. "Why does a warrior stare down a horde of foes just beyond their brothers and sisters in battle? Duty? Bloodthirst? Hard to say for certain."

Esta eased her shoulders and asked, "Why do you know so much?"

Sana folded her hands in her lap, a wistful look in her eyes. "My father was away quite often. He raised me as best he could, but even the First Vampire has his limits. With my mother far off on the plane of Lethe, I had only the comfort of books to raise what my father could not. I don't resent him for it, that would be selfish of me, but I do wonder what could have been if he was around more."

Sana paused and asked, "What of your father, Esta? I have heard more than enough about your brother for one night."

Esta smiled. "First, before anything, my father was a soldier. Every man of the Desidarius carries the weight of the sword. He would often say. He was driven and loyal to those he loved, almost to a fault. Never really knew anything more of him. He expected much out of me, being his eldest daughter."

"How many siblings do you have?"

"Four. Two older brothers, my twin, and my younger sister."

Sana nodded. "What of your sister?"

Esta shook her head. "She was only a child when I was exiled, barely shared a memory with her. The only memories I have with my siblings are of my brothers. I can only hope my sister doesn't repeat my mistakes. The difference between Delsaran and me, other than the obvious, is that I could not break the traditions. I was only able to bend them."

Sana smiled. "There's a scholar in you yet, Diminaire."

Esta chuckled. "Don't be so certain. There's still plenty of libraries to burn."

Drawing her mind away from recent events, Esta asked, "What did Vedus want back in Alrizhod?"

She let out a long sigh. "He… attempted to assassinate me."

Esta nodded. "Okay… any *particular* reason why he's not chained up? Or dead?"

"We still need him, whether we like it or not, which is the only reason why he is alive. I could see it in his eyes. He will not attempt such a thing in the future, at least not until our mission is done. After which, I will ensure that he woefully regrets his attempt."

Esta stood up, tossed her handful of sand down the dune, and shook her head. "And I directed him right to you...."

"It's not your fault–"

"Of course, it is, Sana! I *knew* something was off, and I still let him find you. This is the third time that I've brought your life in danger. If I were you, I'd get as far away from me as possible."

Sana stood and raised her hands. "You're not your brother, Esta. You can't bear the weight of his responsibility."

Esta snapped her head to face Sana. "Because I'm too weak, right?"

Sana shook her head. "That's not your weight to bear. I've seen you do impressive things. Killing Viscerans is not a small feat."

Esta clenched her hand, the sting of her wound rising again. "All I see are vain attempts to repeat my brother's glory."

Sana shrugged. "If you know they're in vain, then why do you attempt at all?"

Esta breathed out, easing her rising anger. "It's better than facing nothingness."

Sana stepped in close, grabbed both of her cheeks, and leaned her down to kiss her forehead.

Esta leaned back. "What was that for?"

Still holding Esta's cheeks, Sana gave a warm smile. "For saving my life when we escaped the Arteries. I never properly thanked you. You're a strong and capable warrior."

Moving one of her hands, Sana leaned in and kissed Esta's right cheek. "That is for leading the Sanguinaire against the Skithik in Alrizhod when I could not be there. You are a wise ruler."

She leaned in and kissed Esta's left cheek. "I never had any siblings, but I am proud of you, and I hope you can accept me as I see you, a sister."

Playing all of the memories they shared in her mind, Esta failed to see Sana as anything less. For one blissful moment, she let go of the pain she had felt for so long.

Sighing with content, Esta replied, "There's a saying amongst the Diminaire, 'All are brothers and sisters under the shower of arrows. All are family behind the shield wall. All are one, with swords facing their shared enemy.' I would be honoured to call you as such."

Sana pulled her into a hug. "This will not be the last time you will face your Sangilis. I can only hope that you can remember your strength when you do. Your strength is not what made you before; despite all the suffering you endured, you stand tall. Your scars are not signs of weakness. Your scars are memorials of your triumph."

Esta returned the hug and whispered, "There's a scholar in you yet."

Chapter Twenty-Seven: Despair of The Wounded Prince

Raking against his armoured form, the desert winds threatened to peel the flesh from his bones. Cutting greedily into his skin. Vedus trudged through heavy sands, making his way to Zelekriv. It was not stubbornness that spurned him to go to Zelekriv but determined that he would achieve victory over the lizard abominations.

As he walked, he heard the shadows warp near him, and Vastra said, "So you're just turning yourself over to the Skithik?"

Vedus answered without looking at her, "That's the idea, yeah."

"Vedus, that's *suicide.*"

"What difference does it make? I've already died. I have nothing else to lose. After all, I'm just a pawn to be used, so it doesn't matter whose side I choose. For once… I would want to carve my own path."

Vastra paused for a moment, then finally said, "We are all the pawns of the Living Shadow and the Eternal Light. There is no respite for the forces of good and evil. If it is death that you crave, then why have you not taken matters into your own hands."

Vedus stopped in his tracks. His gaze invited fear as he said, "Why? So you can deliver my soul to your mother yourself?"

"So you can live a life without fear."

Vedus charged towards Vastra and shouted, "My life is only fear! Every time I close my eyes, I see *him* with his long sharp blade, my family's blood still dripping from the weapon. I can see the hate in his eyes. I can feel the blade gliding over my exposed throat. There is never a moment when I don't think about that day, and what I could have done differently, how my life would have changed if I had chosen not to attend the ceremony. I have never wished death upon myself more than anything in my life."

He pushed past her and continued on his way.

***

Cresting the dune, he found his prize, the last bastion in the desert. Cradled by jagged and jutting mountain crags lied the stone city of Zelekriv.

Even in the low light of the coming twilight, he could see the hideous form resting against the mountains. The gargantuan form of Aaldir, the former God of Blood and lineage. His eyes and cheeks were sunken in, his skin pale and tight upon his desiccated frame. Minutes passed without a single breath releasing from it. It wore a solid black and red tunic stained with his blood from centuries ago. He could almost see it fester.

Dotted around him were sandstone buildings stained with his blood. Warm lights emanated from within. Zelekriv did not sleep, it seemed. Always active, always alert. As he approached the city, he noticed the runes etched along the edges of the walls and the buildings. They were sanctifying wards to protect and guide them.

Approaching the gate, he saw one of the Skithik scrambles to open it. As it opened, there was a throng of lizards waiting for him.

Two burly guards stopped him as they hissed, "You are not permitted to enter the city."

Vedus's tone was even despite his frustration, "I would speak to your leaders."

"And speak you shall." Approaching him was a familiar face.

She stood tall amongst her cold-blooded fellow citizens.

Two joined her, an elderly male lizard that studied Vedus from head to toe and bowed, "Good evening, Prince Vedus. I trust that you are here of your own volition."

His voice rumbled and hissed as the words left his toothy maw.

The other was an elderly female Visceran sporting the same white scales as the other Visceran and said, "There have been no reports about any approaching groups of upstarts."

The familiar one nodded and said, "I am Thras, one of the few Visceran Blood-Seers. These are my colleagues Gorsche and Yudra. What is it you wish to speak to us about?"

He shook his head and said, "I regret to inform you that I do not have terms of their surrender. I am here to turn myself over."

They were taken aback for a moment, unprepared for such news. It took the silence of those around to arouse suspicion.

Gorsche was not impressed or convinced despite the influence he was making on his mind. His psychic energy was not nearly as impressive as Sana's. He could do well for himself.

Thas said, "This slave is handing over to us a great weapon against the Wretched."

Vedus remained quiet as they discussed his fate.

They thought for a moment, then in their hideous tongue, Thras pointed towards him and said, *"Chain him. Bring him to the Demon."*

***

Casting him to the cold floor in a cold, dank room. They pulled the armour off of him, despite the soul-binding nature of it. He felt naked, exposed. The whispers of the shadows were muted for the time being. They seemed to fall silent to the one that he was brought before.

He stood four metres tall, dark ebony black scales with crimson-tinted violet eyes. They promised great pain upon him. Fear had never crept and festered within him before, not since the Night of the Black Swords.

In a low voice that shook the room, it sneered and said, "What filth have you brought before me today?"

The Visceran, Thras, said, "This is an offering from the rebel vampires. They have given him over as a hostage."

A satisfying click rolled through its thick throat as it lumbered towards Vedus.

He shrunk and pushed to go elsewhere, anywhere that was not near him.

Carelessly, he hoisted Vedus to his feet. A firm titanic grip upon his throat choking the life from him. He could feel his vision begin to grow cloudy at the outer edges of his eyes. Only one word came out of his maw as he said, "Why?"

Remaining true to the plan, he choked out, "Fruitless... re... bellion... must... save... self."

The smile remained, and his grip loosened to allow air to rush back into his throat and lungs. Releasing his throat, he instead grabbed him by the hair and pulled him up.

He gazed deep into his eyes, and the prince trembled with a deep feeling of despair.

"I will *enjoy* torturing you."

Casting him back to the floor, he pounced upon Vedus as he skidded across the floor and swiped at him. Two slashes, one along his calf and the other along his left rib. They jolted with activity, and he yelled in pain. His veins ignited with fiery pain as the talons sank deep. He could feel them festering. The muscles contracted and tightened. It became harder and harder to breathe.

As he slowly lost consciousness, he heard the dark-scaled lizard, "What you are feeling is the venom that I have perfected over the last few centuries. You are right now experiencing the first stage of the venom. This will cause all of your muscles to seize and to cease function. Coupled with the feeling that your veins are on fire. Your skin will think that you are burning when you are not. The second stage, the second stage, is the longest. The venom will start to affect your mind. You will see things that aren't there. You will feel things that are not real. While you hallucinate, your flesh softens to the degree that can cause your blood to overproduce. In doing you a favour, I will cut you and let you bleed out.

"The third stage is when the cold grip of death sets in, and itchy frost that never satisfies no matter what you do. It will drive you mad until you start to tear chunks of skin off your flesh. This leads to the fourth and final stage, where all motor and brain functions cease to persist. You will forget everything you are and everyone you love, and every memory will be a distant blur of information you know nothing about, letting you die without your brain dying and your heart stopping. And when confusion sets in and you forget who you are. Fear makes the blood taste all the more sweet."

He began to fade in and out of consciousness. In each flash, he was dragged down some hallway. Whether from the venom or the phosphorus that burned on the torches, the lights were a dark red. Hope left once he saw it, the hanging iron hook that promised more pain than he had ever experienced before.

He could hear them gently whispering, murmuring and talking amongst themselves. He knew their habits and how they would react.

He was drenched in sweat, mixing with blood trailing behind him. This was a common way to tend to his victims as he felt the caked blood underneath his back. Vedus trembled with pain, his muscles seizing.

White hot brands clamped onto his shoulders as the dark-scaled Skithik grabbed and hoisted him up. The voices laughed and cheered as he was lowered onto the hook. He stared long into the Skithik's eyes, savouring his agony as the iron hook pierced through his flesh with ease. He gasped as he was hanging onto the meat hook. He howled in pain, the maddening tone of his voice joining the choir of black voices that threatened to overtake his mind.

Seizing his jaw with a yelp escaping his lips, it said, "My name is Telrokas. I am death. I am a *God*. I will pry every last shred of information and mortality out of your mind. I am not going to make things easy for you. I am going to ask you questions, and if I find your answer unsatisfactory or I am growing bored, I will increase the pain I will inflict upon you. I am going to make you beg for death. I will make you wish that you resided within the deepest pit of Nosgora. For the devils are more forgiving than I."

The air rippled with an ear-shattering shriek that mixed with the maddening laughs and wails of the shadows. Vedus slipped into unconsciousness.

Chapter Twenty-Eight: The Walls of Zelekriv

Sana

The wizened Sanguinaire recalled the triumphant revolution of the Skithik against the Ilthauns. It was ironic how thousands of years later, they were the ones being revolted against. Perhaps it was just the passing of history that there will always be tyrants to squash. Their city was named after the revolution against the Ilthauns, the Zelekriv. In the lizard's tongue, it meant; the want of blood. The Dwarves referred to it as the Illithaun War, but that was not until the elves broke free as well.

The sands hungered for blood. Sana could feel it in the air. So much blood had already been shed, but oceans were needed to retake their rightful place. Zeal coursed through her veins and the zeal she imprinted on her citizens. Their faces spoke of the same hunger for vengeance she craved to steal the blood from the lizard imposters. Stealing powers that belonged to the Children of Silthar.

They marched through the muck, through sand, their steps guiding them towards the awaiting blood of the enemy. Long have they waited for this moment, she could feel the eagerness in their minds. Their hands itched to spill blood, the blood of their enemies.

She focused her mind upon Esta, whom she knew was still struggling to maintain her Sangilis. Behind the rows of skeletons she marched with, she could see Esta in the front row of the contingent that would climb the peaks and descend upon the unwitting defenders of Zelekriv. She hungered for their blood, though not to the same degree as all the others. She knew if she indulged the blood-crazed spirit that riled within her, she entertained the idea of becoming primal. All was well so far. She just hoped Esta could maintain control over it.

Nothing stopped them. There was no pause as they trudged through sand to the accursed city of degenerate filth. Long had she waited for this moment, her shared vengeance against the Skithik was also present. She could not endure the cruel image that they took any longer. They tarnished the name and the ways of the vampire to satisfy their icons of cruelty. To kill your own God out of selfishness and lust for power sickened her. What afterlife awaited them? Nothing pleasant, not that Sana cared.

They were a few miles outside of Zelekriv. Sana took a deep breath as the plan unfolded. They marched towards the walls of Zelekriv, hoisting the banners and heads of the

Skithik they had killed. As they marched, the other contingent of vampires sneaked through the shadows and crept along with the dark blanket of night.

She could hear them, their cries and hisses of anger and pain. She could listen to them distantly stirring. They readied themselves for a battle that they were not prepared to fight. Unhitched, their plan was beginning to bear fruit. She ordered them to pick up the pace and divert to the right as she saw the gates open. She watched as piling out in droves were Skithik warriors, blood-crazed and ready to die for their vampire overlords.

Sana ordered them to sprint, continuing their path. Arrows began to rain from the sky. Alight with tongues of orange flames as they sailed through the sky towards them. Since they were arrows, it did bother the skeletons. The necromancers that joined them were forced to use magical shields to defend against the arrows. While they could withstand damage from fire, they were still susceptible to it.

They charged on through the initial wave. Sana whipped her head back as they continued their tireless charge diverting from the walls of Zelekriv. As they assumed, the gate was still open. The arrows ceased their volley as they were too far away; as they reached the end of the arrow's reach, she ordered them to tighten ranks quickly and counter-charge the Skithik.

The skelctons barked and hissed, their simple minds ready to rend through living flesh. She could see the horror-stricken faces of some of the Skithik warriors. They looked upon the torn skin of their brethren, the severed heads, and the skeletons tinged red with the blood of the Skithik. Bathing in the blood of fallen foes during a war was a common practice of the Sanguinaire. It struck fear into the hearts of their enemies in hopes they would surrender. The Skeletons' eyes bore ethereal red motes of magical energy. Telling all of their power to raise the dead. She even gave orders to raise the fallen Skithik to further strike fear into them.

Steel met steel as the forces of the Children of Silthar and the Skithik clashed. Ill-prepared to deal with skeletons, they foolishly advanced. The smell of blood rose high on the desert winds. The gate and walls of Zelekriv were in sight. Past the raging soldiers of the night, she saw the forest of arrows. Their fire leeched unto the sand and solidified into red glass. Sana took note of this and continued with the battle.

Casting a spell, she summoned her shadow blade and with a few words, the air warped and distorted for a moment.

Scarlet red energy burst to life in the centre of the Skithik. She requested the aid of some of the necromancers near her, and they offered their aid.

Using the borrowed energy, she created a ball of writhing and swirling energy much larger than she was. It growled as it remained stationary. As blood soaked the sand, the swirling red energy would pulsate, and a brief shockwave would erupt. This would hopefully distract some of them to get more to fall to the blades of their skeletal warriors.

They were steadily winning the battle when she looked and saw riding out swift creatures that bore some of the elite Visceran.

They strode atop beastly raptors that gnashed and hissed in the night air. They burst from the gates and strode towards them. They were fast and were in good numbers. If they charged them, the Song of War would sing in their favour. She ordered a few of the necromancers to divert from the main body and focus with her on the charging mobile units of the Skithik.

Her eyes erupted with hungry dark energy, and her sword danced in the shadowy light. The wind picked up as she called upon the powers of the dark. They answered to her, forcing her will upon the resting shadows. The writhing spirits of the dead awakened once more and sailed through the air towards the charging cavalry.

The necromancers let loose volleys of green eldritch energy that wailed as they readied to strike their enemies. As the spirits sailed, she connected her magical will to the sailing motes of green necrotic energy, and they surged with power.

They burst and lapped the cavalry, leeching necrotic energy as they struck their targets. The spirits lashed out as well and slowed their charge. Gliding across the shadows, Sana countercharged; wreathed herself in scarlet energy as they ceased their charge to strike at formless foes.

She joined the fray, lashing with her sword and tongues of her red energy. She could feel the steady stream of magic the necromancers gave to her wreathing magic; all was going well. The blood leapt without abandon through the air. Before it would soak into the sand, it would suspend in the air for a moment and then she would absorb it. The pandemonium was glorious.

Two Visceran braved the storm of vampiric magic and readied their weapons to strike, one with a spear and the other with a curved cavalry sword.

The one with the cavalry sword charged first, raising their sword high. She parried it as it came down, hoping its "superior" strength would do enough to impose upon her. When she did not flinch, his stance changed to a more defensible one as she unleashed an unrelenting assault of strikes against him. His battle stance was good, and he struggled to keep up with her, but he did.

The spear thrust from behind the sword-wielding one as the strike connected. She dodged at the last second, the spearhead marking her armour along her navel. In a downward stroke, her magical blade severed the top of the spear. As the pole disappeared behind the other Skithik, he leapt towards the other, her sword poised.

Before the spearhead could fall to the sand, she grabbed it with her left hand. As she parried and deflected the strike to the side, she stepped in closer to the Visceran and plunged the spearhead deep into its side. It howled in pain; she cut the strap holding up its breastplate using the opportunity.

It recovered from the strike and joined the stride of the other Visceran that now drew its own cavalry sword.

A sadistic smile crept along her face as she willed the spilling blood to take shape. It stopped and then slowly crept back into its body.

She watched as its blood began to turn black, its veins starkly visible against its white scales. It collapsed to its knees, dropping its sword as it screamed in pain. The other could only look on in horror, realising all she needed was a single wound to kill.

Black ichorous blood drained from its eyes and maw. Steam rolled from every pore of its body as it fell limply to the blood-soaked sand.

The terrified Skithik shook as it readied its blade and said in common, "What are you?"

She replied, tasting the blood from her blade, and said, "The vengeance of Silthar."

Chapter Twenty-Nine: Blood from the Mountains

Esta

The snowfall drafted against their ebony cloaks, covering their tracks and shrouding them in misty ice winds. The cold nipped at the edges of her cloth but went no further, not that she could feel the bitter cold temperature. The veiled winds changed them, appearing as blackened spectres.

Blacksun's runes were wreathed in a red mist. The dark blade hungered for blood, just as she and the rest of her retinue did. Presiding within the walls of Zelekriv, they were awaiting foes to shower them in their blood. The memory of Skithik blood danced across her tongue; she was eager to drink from them.

With the wind howling against the mountaintops, she almost did not hear Alaric, who said, "Too cruel a thing to catch your enemy unaware. Not cruel enough if your blade passes them."

Esta nodded and said, "The words of warrior-poet Silandris, from his seminal piece '*The Long and Distant Battlefield.*'"

Alaric spoke evenly, comfortably trudging the weight of vampirism, "We studied many works of past warriors. Your ancestor Vcralldin Desidarius was another one."

Esta spoke, *"To begin the morning with freshly spilled blood is to offer the kindest bounties to the awaiting Pantheon."*

Alaric nodded, a small smile on his face. He wore black steel plate armour, wrapping over his warfare-sculpted frame. He was a knight; the weight was familiar to him. The scarlet eyes and the hunger for blood were not. Two swords were strapped to his left side, with a quiver of javelins resting on his waistline. His face told stories, many knights did. There was comfort in his eyes, with pain just below the surface. His short black, swept hair gently waved in the howling wind as he said, "Though you likely grow tired of hearing about the great successes of your lineage."

Esta spoke earnestly to the turned knight and said, "They are a source of my strength. We were taught from a young age always to remember the warriors of our past. Gain wisdom from their successes and insight into their failures. The weight of ghosts has no bearing on who I am."

"And what of your brother, Ezran?"

She paused for a moment as they came to a rock shelf; just past the veil of winter winds sweeping against the mountainside, they could see the wounded form of Aaldir. As they stopped, she scoured the winds for an answer. Had she moved past his strangulating shadow?

The half-elf spoke from the heart again, "His legends continue the legacy of my living family. My bond is to those sired to me. They are my family now."

His smile faded as he joined her side against the cliff. Looking down, the vast wall that enclosed the body of Aaldir could be seen. The forms that patrolled them were almost invisible to their eyes.

Esta stabbed her runeblade into the stone and peered out through the veil to the wide desert just below the sheer cliffs of the mountains. Blasted forests and ruined grassy knolls clawed at the bottoms of the mountain, past that was the vast desert of Urstron. Scholars believe Urstron was once part of Seranetis but was severed from the mainland long ago.

Alaric said, "Have they begun their decoy?"

Esta nodded, "The gate remains open, but I have not found them yet."

"I pray they have not taken them too far."

The Lord-Sire hoped as much. However, she knew that battle changes the plans of invasion often. Only on a few occasions does an invasion go exactly according to plan. Improvisation was needed for the pandemonium of war.

She finally spotted them at the crest of where the mountains met at a point. Sana wreathed in necrotic energy as she lit up the battlefield with her unique swordsmanship. Expressing her expertise at blade dancing.

They waited until they saw the cavalry careen out of the city gate, charging towards the battle.

Esta burst to her feet and ordered, "We fall out now! Descend upon them! Leave no trace of their existence! Wipe them from history!"

They bellowed against the arctic winds as they descended from the mountains, sliding against the sheer cliffs of the mountains. Some landed on the wall, Esta and Alaric included. Others, led by Zelphar, made it into the city proper to begin ransacking it.

Feet touched paved sandstone and charged for the gatehouse. Forming an arch over the gate was the gatehouse that controlled its movements. If they could handle that and maintain control, victory would be assured.

Skithik mobilised and scattered to try to repel the shadows descending from the mountain, but they were ill-prepared. Sweeping a Skithik off their feet, she plunged the blade and her foe into the stone below her, showering her ebony armour in fresh blood. Blacksun hummed with satisfaction as it drank the essence from her fallen foe.

Coming to the arch, Skithik rangers raised their bows against them. Esta ordered them all to take cover. The first volley took out a few of her soldiers; the rest braced against the cover. Once the first volley was done, they charged a few metres from the bottom of the arch and descended upon them.

Her slash severed their bow in half, and before they had time to unsheathe their weapon to defend themselves, she cleaved through them with ease.

Minutes passed, and Skithik after Skithik rose to defend the gatehouse, but they all succumbed to Esta's bloodline warriors.

They cleared the large gatehouse and secured all entrances and exits. Esta flicked her blade, painting the stone floor with blood.

She peered out and saw the cavalry falling to the skeletal battalion led by Sana and the necromancers. Sana was making quick work of them and soon tightened their ranks and began to march towards Zelekriv.

Esta smiled as she shouted, "Keep the gate open."

The battle was underway. The two forces of the Sanguinaire met at the gate as the Skithik formed ranks inside. The armies met and exchanged dead, Sana and Esta fought next to one another, and blood filled the air. The Skithik that did not partake in blood were no match for their supernatural fury.

The half-elf blood lord estimated they did not last more than an hour. The only thing that saved them was the silver weaponry they had at their disposal.

Thrusting her blade deep into her last foe, she wrenched the blade from the lifeless lizard and looked at the scene before her. Caked in freshly spilled blood, bodies of the Skithik filled the desert floor. A handful of Sanguinaire soldiers mixed in, but they still held comfortable numbers. Bones scattered about.

Fires had begun to be lit, and the buildings within the city began to be set aflame. Then they heard the cries of the Skavarn, their rapturous calls gathering the attention of the Sanguinaire forces.

Esta ordered them to tighten their ranks, and the skeletons formed in front with the Sanguinaire on their side, creating a chevron.

They watched as towering Skavarn warriors' ranks formed amongst the burning buildings. Their hideous forms were hungry for blood, their teeth stained with the fresh blood of their God. Before Esta had time to think, she bellowed a mighty warcry, and her Snaguinaire hissed in agreement toward her, countercharging the rushing forces of the Skavarn.

Her blade made the gleaming silver weapons of a Skavarn warrior once more, and they exchanged blows for quite some time. It was fast, but she was faster. The well-trained warrior backhanded against her sturdy plate armour, flesh and bone bursting against her magically infused armour. With the pommel of her sword, she connected it with the side of the Skavarn warrior's head, causing it to fall to the ground.

Raising her sword to deflect the blow of another warrior's blade, she unleashed a burst of magic that sent it stumbling back. She plunged her sword deep into the Skavarn at her feet, twisting her dark blade in its flesh, churning the blood within. The blood rose with life and formed a barrier as a warrior clashed against it.

Esta pulled her sword from her fallen foe and saw Sana as she exchanged blows with a Skavarn and outstretched her arm to form the barrier. With a flick of her wrist, she showered the blood against the whitewashed scales of the Skavarn warriors. They cried out in anger.

The Skavarn were making quick work of the skeleton soldiers, as they expected. The Sanguinaire posed the real challenge. The air sang with unique cruelty as vampires clamoured to kill vampires. The abominable Skithik struck with a ferocity that the Sanguinaire could not match, but they offered more uniform strikes as they all connected to the psyche of Sana. She issued orders and fixated their minds on the spilling of their blood.

The battle was long, they pushed the Skavarn, and they pushed back. They proved they would not die so easily. A sandstorm swept across the city of Zelekriv and beat against the warriors. The Sanguinaire used the sandstorm to their advantage and hid amongst the whipping grains of sand. Esta could feel her Sangilis growing impatient as she joined the pulling Sanguinaire forces.

She struck with renewed vigor and a taste for the victory ahead. They did not fall with the Skithik they dealt with as much, but they still succumbed to her dark blade. Her heart beat loudly in her ears, her veins alight with the promise of death and pain to her foes. Her fangs extended, and anger bellowed from her scarlet eyes. She shook as her Sangilis fought for control of her actions. The darkened soul, tainted with necrotic magic, pawed at her sanity.

Her vision was almost filled with red as she could feel the invading strength of her Sangilis. Most of the Sanguinaire around her had no such weaknesses. They were all fledglings with their Sangilis's dormant.

"Remember something special to you."

Esta spat, *"It's almost taken control…."*

"What is the one memory you hold most dear?"

In her mind, she remembered back to a memory she always thought back to when the blood-rage of battle threatened to overtake her in hopes of quieting her Sangilis. When she was smaller, when she and Ezran were children and first took up the sword. They practised near the edge of their clan village.

Ezran always won. This particular moment filled Esta with rage and unleashed her anger on him. Their aunt, Salasti, their instructor, stopped their sparring and said, *"Do not allow your mind to become clouded by your emotions. Recklessness can carry you far in a duel, but it will not always carry you to victory. Calm strikes fear in the heart of your enemies more than your rage."*

Esta's red vision faded. Breathing heavily, she looked down at Blacksun and the bodies scattered around her. None of those kills were guided by her hand. They were all guided by Blacksun. Easing the adrenaline in her veins, her Sangilis quieted.

As the battle waned, she looked about the battlefield before them. The skeleton soldiers were all fallen and joined the dead, with the remaining necromancers moving to resurrect them with unlife once more. They had two-thirds the number of Sanguinaire soldiers, keeping the tide of battle in their favor.

The remaining Skavarn retreated to the keep and assured the Sanguinaire victory of control over the buildings within the city. Sana and Esta looked at one another; their crusade was nearly done. The only deed left was to slay the leadership that presided within the keep of Zelekriv. They could feel the satisfaction of Silthar as they ordered the bulk of their forces to stay in the city and defend against any approaching Skithik from the desert. They took a small entourage of fifty Sanguinaire and charged towards the keep.

Blacksun and Esta both hummed with gleeful anticipation.

Chapter Thirty: The Blood Runs Cold

Vedus trembled as he regained consciousness. The fugue state he found himself in was torturous. The reality he saw was not real, but that did not stop his mind from telling him otherwise. The walls were peeling away, revealing the empty oblivion that lay beyond.

The pain was too much; it was the bulk of the reason why he would slip from consciousness. His muscles were singed with the white-hot fury of pain. He would say that he was on his way to being sore, but they did not feel as though they were healing. They weighed a great ton upon his bones.

In that fugue state, he heard *her* voice, *"You poor thing. To receive such treatment is mortifying."*

Vedus painfully shook his head, gasps, living and dying on his breath as he said, "No… you're not… real."

He felt a gust of cold wind step closer to him, and a force lifted his chin slowly. He winced at the pain of such a simple action and saw her.

It was the queen of shadows herself, Satris. Her skin was a pleasant shade of blue, expressing her strange undead state. Curved horns protruded from her head, framing the gold headdress she wore. The regalia as well was glimmering in the dim light. A necklace wrapped around her neck snugly, and decorative bracelets. She wore a gown of shadows that congealed into her form and joined the writhing shadows upon her lower half.

His heart began to race as he said with wide eyes, "No… it can't… be."

Satris leaned in, her breath husky and low, as she said, "Oh, but I can. While I might not be able to manifest fully unto the mortal plane of existence, I can manifest a portion of myself. When I heard what you were enduring, I had to come and find you, my poor little prince."

He stared long into her large red eyes, similar to his vampire companions. Yet these were different. There was hunger behind Esta's and Sana's eyes. A deep primal hunger with no satisfaction. Behind Satris's eyes were desire and temptation. They welcomed him to join in their vastness. In any other state, he would have had the strength of will to resist her.

He was so tired. His muscles were so sore that they were the only thing he could think about. His desire to end this pain caused his mind to succumb to her throes. His eyes grew wide as he accepted the dark magic to overtake his thoughts, his mind grew numb, and the only thing he could think about was to satisfy her. For a brief moment, he forgot the venom that coursed through his veins and was killing him. Everything was secondary to her.

Her smile lit up his soul as she said, still gazing deep into his eyes, "There's the subservience I love to see."

He gasped as he replied, "What do you require of me, my queen?"

Any resistance died in his mind. Her grasp that she had upon his mind was so great that he forgot where he was and what he was doing. He craved to serve her; there was nothing that would satisfy him more than serving her every whim.

She stepped back, gently gliding over the floor. The queen of shadows looked him up and down and grew slightly offended, likely not at anything he did, more so at the state he was in.

Satris daintily waved her hand, gesturing up and down at him, and said, "Relieve yourself of this state. The fact that these abominations have the gall to torture one of my warlocks is beyond my understanding. Drawing the ire of two Gods is not wise; then again, this is the same group of mortals that killed their own to grab power."

As she spoke, he forced himself off the meat hook; as he slid against the iron hook, he felt his consciousness slip. Pain shot through his back and his chest, his arms shaking as his body begged him to remain at rest. Tears welled in his eyes as the icy hot venom surged through his muscles. Yet he pressed on. He needed to do this. Anything to not anger the queen of shadows. Slowly he pressed through and fell to the floor with a thud. He trembled with great pain, his muscles slowly but surely adjusting back to the state they used to be in when he was not impaled upon the hook.

She leaned down, lifting his left arm. He raised his head, sweat dripping from the top of his brow, cold sweat soaking him. He took deep breaths and did not waver or flinch under her gaze. She had his undivided attention. "Such strength. I have not felt such unprecedented power from another mortal before. You are truly a living testimony of strength, power, and will."

He bowed his head, nearly weeping at her compliments, "You honour me, my queen."

Her mood shifted as she continued, causing his breath to catch in his throat, "Why then do you squander it engaging yourself with my daughter? If it were any of my other daughters, I would be fine, but Vastra? She speaks only in lies and deceit. She has only herself in mind. She will use you and then cast you away... and that is no way to treat one such as you."

She reached her hand closer to him, drawing her fingers over his cheek. He could feel her tugging at his soul. He offered no resistance as she pawed at the ancient energy that kept him alive and said as she investigated his soul, "Such a unique soul. Souls themselves are quite unique, I find. There is no other magical energy quite like it. The Gods bathe themselves in it, allowing themselves to drown in their vanity."

He felt no words, his breath catching as she tugged at it. She was delighted at it and said, "While you might think that your soul is tainted because of the state you found yourself in, I can assure you it is as pure as I found it when I plucked it from the afterlife."

He paused for a moment as his muscles quivered with pain that rivalled no other. Falling to his hands and knees, he belted a cry of pain so intense he felt the room shake with his cry of misery.

She let go of the strands of his soul and said, lifting him back up, "You are in a great deal of pain, and you will die."

He shook his head violently, pleading to her as he said, "No, please. Not again. I won't go back again!"

Sympathy drenched her aeons' lost face as she said, "I know, my little darling. I know. I would not wish to have you return to dust."

She pulled him closer to her; her cold skin was quite inviting. They soothed his irritated muscles and calmed his mind to an extent. Bliss rolled off of his shoulders like a mantle of nirvana.

She whispered in his ear, "I can *cure* you. I can drive away the poison that flows through your veins."

He nodded his head furiously, hugging her tighter as he pleaded, "Yes! Please! Anything!"

With a voice that rivalled the choirs of the heavens itself, she whispered in his ear, "You must swear yourself to me and me *only*."

He nodded, and she continued, "With these words, I solidify our pact. Under the witnesses of the shadows themselves, I humbly accept your offer, and in return, I shall give power everlasting. You shall be my conduit on this wounded plane. You shall live without any fear or regret of this pact."

She pushed against him and looked deep into his eyes; his heart fluttered for a moment as she asked, "Do you accept these terms? Will you give me your soul in exchange for life and power?"

There was no pause for reflection as he said, "Yes, thank you, please. You will not regret this. I will serve you loyally until the end of my days."

She smiled, warming his heart and soul as she said, "Well, aren't you sweet."

Cupping his cheeks, she leaned in and pressed her lips against his.

For a moment, they were warm, and it was the most delightful kiss he had ever experienced as time drew on, though the cold set in once more. His muscles healed, and his mind cleared for a moment before it slipped away. Dreaded realisation set in. He just gave his soul to the queen of succubi. Willingly.

Those defiant thoughts died as soon as they lived, as he now felt a distinct emptiness. He felt drained, accepting the cold oblivion. He felt his psyche adjust to the void, he drank in its breadth. Then, he felt complete again. Intense emotions rose and fell like the tides of the ocean. He fell to his hands and knees once more.

He could feel their hands pawing at him, gently gliding over his form as they lifted him. He kept his eyes closed as he entered a state of bliss beyond compare. The Queen of Shadow's first gift to him. They raised him up and moaned in despair at his pain.

"You remember the cambions I gave you, don't you? My first order is for you to cleanse this plane of the blight that is the Skithik. And then, you will find and kill your rebellious father. He stands as a mockery of my power."

While he hovered slowly in the air, he felt Vallia, Savine, Dalia, and Salaia put varying armour pieces upon his form. He could hear their delighted voices as they had an excuse to touch him once more.

When the last piece was upon him, he drifted back to the floor, the armour bonded with him. It was lightweight and conformed to his shape. It felt just like when Satris embraced him. It felt only natural for such armour to be worn.

He knelt, the plate clattering as he did so.

"Now raise your hands and accept my last gift."

Raising his hands, he felt as the air shifted, and he felt a blade materialise into his hands.

It had the appearance of an elvish longsword, the curved blade was undeniable. True to the make of elvish weaponry, there was no pommel or crossguard. There was no weight to drawback strikes, making it one of the deadliest weapons on Calisine. Elvish swordmasters were among the most intensely trained, second only to the half-elven blade masters.

The sword gleamed with polished silver light. It shined as if it was a solidified ray of moonlight. The grey, slightly curved, and polished hilt held the image of a posing woman embossed under the polished surface. Intricate inlays danced the length of the blade, Reyluneaux. The elves used the intricate flowing language of runes to tell a story with their blade and bless it with magical abilities.

The blade felt a part of him, and him a part of the blade. It felt perfect as he wrapped his fingers around it. They were one.

He nodded to Satris and said, "I will christen this blade with the blood of the Skithik."

Vedus opened his eyes and saw he was in an empty room; looking about, he was in a vast stone room. The cold air of the dungeon he found himself in accepting him. Rising to his feet, he felt his muscles rejuvenated by the powers of his patron. For once, since his resurrection, he felt driven. He felt purpose. He felt whole.

He let go of the blade and watched as it disappeared. He raced out of the room, ready to find the Skithik and coat the walls with their blood.

***

300

Esta and Sana burst through the door to the innermost chamber of the keep. Their breaths were long and laborious. In the halls, they heard the sound of clashing steel and cries of war. They assured themselves that their Sanguinaire could handle themselves as they found the Skithik leadership.

Esta looked to Sana, flicking her blade and painting the stone floor with the blood of its citizens. "Where could they have taken Vedus? Can you sense him?"

Sana reached out for a moment, drinking in the energies that gave her power. A minute or so passed, and a puzzled expression crossed her face.

"What is it?" Esta asked.

Sana shook her head, "I can feel him within the walls of the keep, but he is... *different*...."

"Different how?"

"I suspect it has something to do with his bond to the Queen of Shadows."

Esta knew whom she was referring to, though she dared not speak her name lest she was listening in the shadows. All someone needed to do was say her name, and she would appear. With a gaze alone, she could collapse entire empires.

The Lord-Sire shook her head, "Has he made his pact with her?"

Sana pursed her lips, "I can only assume."

Esta sighed with frustration, "What will we do with him?"

They paused their conversation as they stepped further into the room. It served as a throne room and a council room. Five thrones decorated the back wall between the two archways leading further into the keep. All were made of bones and upholstered with dried, leathery skin. It was grotesque; then again, Esta did not assume that the Skithik were among the nobler folk. Another reason to hate them beyond their blight upon the nature of vampires.

Sana continued as she looked about the tapestries that hung high above their heads, "We will decide what to do later. For the moment, we need him to kill the Skithik leaders."

As she spoke those words, Esta and Sana dashed out of the way of streams of magic that staggered across the room in fractions of seconds. Looking up, they saw the Skithik leadership, four Skavarn dressed in thin robes inlaid with silver and gold. They were bearing regalia made from bone. Their blood-drenched claws outstretched with beams of magical energy, destroying the polished stone floors.

The magic ceased, allowing Esta time to charge forward and raise Blacksun, ready to thrust the blade deep into one of them. It fell into rhythm with her, dodging and weaving away from her sword. Breaking her stride with her sword, as it pierced through a magical barrier they summoned, she pulled out one of her bone daggers and plunged the blade deep into the leader.

Surprisingly, their eyes rolled back, all life draining into Blacksun.

Stunned for a moment, she quickly found cover behind a nearby pillar and said in Sana's mind, *"These aren't the leaders."*

Sana replied, *"I saw; who could the leaders be?"*

Leaping from behind the pillar, she cleaved through each of the Skithik that defiantly attacked them, each absorbing into her hungry blade. Her Sangilis also calmed to a degree. It rested as her zealous fury was not as intense.

Standing amidst blood and death, she flicked her blade as they heard someone speak, "Well played. I was beginning to think that I was not going to face you both."

They turned and saw the first Skithik of this colour, his scales were pitch black. He wore no armour, ragged trousers, and a necklace made from platinum, with amethyst jewels glinting in the low light. He towered above any Skavarn they faced thus far. Power rolled off of his shoulders like death. This was who they were to kill.

It growled and said, "I am Telrokas, the Demon. Leader of the Skithik. And you both must be Sana and Esta, respectively. I have been waiting a long time for us to meet."

Esta shouted and charged; Blacksun raised, "Then why stand on ceremony!"

"I agree."

Each strike, he timed perfectly to dodge and weave. He was fast despite his towering frame. She could not land a strike. Finding an opening in her defences, he collided with the back of his monstrous claw against her. She muscled a portion of his strength and stumbled back. Shaking the confusion from her eyes, she watched as Sana unleashed darts of concentrated magical energy towards Telrokas, each one absorbed into brief barriers of his magical energies.

He smiled darkly as he said, "Let's even the odds."

He pulled a gem from a pouch, crushed it in his titanic grip, and let the gem dust float into the air. He manifested magic for a moment, and the air quickly grew dead with the lack of magical energy. Blacksun went quiet.

Sana summoned her dark blade, and the two Sanguinaire charged him. Fury unleashes upon him pent-up aggression from years of torture and misery. In the back of Esta's mind, she said to herself, *"Wherever you are, Vedus, we need you now."*

With each dodged strike, she could feel the pain of defeat already.

He found the perfect spots to plant his strikes. Palm strikes, balled punches, never once drawing a weapon. He patiently struck them both, wearing them down. No matter how fast, no matter what tactics they used, they could not break his defence. There were times when there was a single clarifying moment that they had their opening, but he would still deflect the blow.

He did not move; all they could do was recover and unleash their fury. They could not even reach their Sangilis. Esta noticed his regalia hummed with a null power. That was the conduit that prevented their magic, but she could not reach it.

In unified complexity, they unleashed furious blows, and both finished with a downward slash. Maddeningly, he caught both blades. He yanked them and pulled them from their grips. The tired Sanguinaire rushed him.

Esta went low, and Sana went high.

Telrokas, masterful as he was, deflected Sana's reaching punch with his elbow and counter-struck with a swift jab to her navel. The wind left her lungs as she fell to the floor past Telrokas.

Esta went to sweep the legs, a mistake as Telrokas lifted his leg and slammed down on hers, stopping the movement. It did not hurt, but she was vulnerable.

Before she could retaliate, he grabbed her by the throat and tightened his grip. He slowly lifted her into the air, and looking at her as she struggled against his strength, he said, "It is futile. You cannot strike me down. You never will. You ill-prepared wretches did not know that you could not kill me, I am a Sanguinaire, and because of a decree of your God, you cannot even land a strike. Your Sangilis forbids it."

Esta spat at the hideous abomination, silently mortified that he was correct. They knew they could do nothing against him; they were only buying time as Vedus found his way to them.

He tightened his grip around her throat, gathering another cough from her as he said, "I will wear you both down until you barely cling to life and make you watch as I annihilate every vampire you have sired to you. Then, I will keep you as my victims to torture for all eternity."

Esta wanted to tell him he was wrong; she wanted to say that he was going to die, that she would personally watch as life drained from him. But that was not the case. Instead, she silently prayed to Silthar that Vedus would be near them soon. Just as the edge of her vision began to fade, she watched as his eyes grew wide for a moment. She heard the sound of steel piercing flesh.

He released his grip, and she went into a coughing fit as she slammed against the stone floor. She was nearly falling with her blood that dotted the floor from their long battle with him.

She looked up and saw a sword that gleamed with the brilliance of moonlight pierced through his chest. Sana recovered from her wound, and the Hands of Silthar looked at each other and watched as life began to drain from Telrokas.

He spat, clinging to life, "This… this is not my end! I was to conquer Calisine! Enoch promised me the throne!"

They felt the air shift and shake as Telrokas's eyes were washed in black, and a dark voice bellowed forth, "You have failed me, Telrokas. You allowed your hubris to cloud your judgement. Now you will die a coward's death at the hands of those that you once enslaved."

"I don't like this…."

Esta stood, wiping blood from her knee. *"Yeah... I can't help but feel like we're giving Enoch exactly what he wants."*

Sana and Esta connected gazes. Sana replied. *"We have killed one of his most prized generals. I consider that a victory."*

All three swords, invigorated with the blessing of Silthar and Enoch, plunged down into Telrokas, who collapsed to his knees. Blood decorated them all as the deed was done.

They cleaned their blades and heard Enoch's final words before his dark essence disappeared, "So, these are the new Hands of Silthar? I must say that you have dealt a great blow to my cause by killing one of my most decorated generals. But that is secondary to the pain I will inflict upon the countryside of Ketos. They will feel my wrath from all that you took from me this day. Enjoy your victory; I invite you to try and kill me."

His essence left, and they all breathed a sigh of relief. Esta looked out the nearby window towards the horizon, equally anxious and fearful to continue their crusade against Enoch the Nocturnal. But it was a victory all the same. She watched the sun as the violet, and blood-red rays painted the sky.

As the sun died, its rays cast gruesome shadows over the flayed dead. Sana said to Esta, *"Telrokas and his blighted kin. The servants of blood, no more, feast upon the pain and misery of the night's children. For we overthrew the abominations of the night and seized their power once more. The children of Silthar are renewed, and now we'll quench our thirst with the blood of the Traitor Hand. The bells toll for the Nocturnal, a crusade will rise to meet him and wipe him from the face of Calisine..."*

"The Sanguinairian War has just begun...."

Epilogue: Children and Their Thrones

Esta looked to Sana, her eyes cooling from the primordial vengeance that flowed from her veins. They exchanged worried glances before Esta said in Sana's mind, *"Vedus remains. What shall we do?"*

Sana breathed, dusting off her cloak as she responded to her sire, *"Fulfil my promise."*

The Heir of Night turned to Vedus and willed her sword into existence. The glimmering shadow blade extended forth, crackling with an icy promise of death.

"You were always one to keep your word."

Sana stole a glance at Esta. The Lord-Sire readied to summon Blacksun, spreading her legs shoulder-width apart.

Sana continued, "Then, if you know me so well, then you know to make this quick for yourself."

Esta looked into Vedus's eyes or what was left of them. There was not even the barest hint of Vedus remaining behind them. His eyes were vacant. His soul has been ferried to the Queen of Shadows to toy with as she chose. It pained her to see her companion in such a state. The room grew dark. The windows shuttered from the rising sun outside. Darkness covered the room.

Esta summoned Blacksun and was about to rush Vedus when a presence entered the room.

A voice rose in the darkness, saying, "Tsk tsk tsk. Now now, noble lord of blood. Do not be so hasty."

Sana joined Esta's side and said, "Keep quiet; let me do the talking."

The presence manifested, and it was none other than Satris, the Shadow Queen herself. Esta had seen her visage in the churches of Uthos, erected amongst the other Gods of the Pantheon. She was the Messenger of the Void. A servant of good and evil.

She sauntered next to Vedus and cooed with a gleeful smile, "Look at the two of you. The Hands of Silthar. Times most certainly are changing. This reminds me that I should pay a visit to Silthar; the poor boy is still wounded from his last encounter with his dear old father."

Esta could feel the restraint of herself and Sana as they wanted to do something to break the hold that Satris had on Vedus. But they feared what would surely follow if they attempted such a thing.

Sana spoke and said, "Why are you here?"

Satris ran a finger over Vedus's jawline and said, "Call it throwing my hat in the ring for the war ahead. From what

I hear, it will shake the foundation of you mortals and those of us on the mountain high. Dear, beautiful, Vedus here will kill his resurrected father for me. Us gods only have so much forethought before we have to… intervene, I suppose?

"Or did you mean why I am here and now? Well, call it a hunch, but I know the reputation that follows with my warlocks to you mortals. You look at them with such hatred, and I cannot help but intervene when they are most threatened. Nosgora knows no fury like a woman scorned. You both know that better than anyone, don't you?"

Esta clenched her fists and said, "Then take your prize and leave."

Satris pressed her fingers to her chest and said with a devilish smile, "My my, look at the defiance on this one. Is that how you treat Silthar? I think not."

Carving into Esta's mind, she felt a cold sting spread across her thoughts, and she slumped to the ground. Sana stood headlong against the psychic waves of pain, unmoved and unphased.

Satris's eyes narrowed as she said as she cocked her head to the side, "I haven't seen a will like that for a long time, young elf."

Sana never faltered her gaze as she replied, "I think you'll find I'm full of surprises."

The Shadow Queen smiled and said, "Children and their thrones… as fun as that sounds, unfortunately, I don't have time to turn both of your brains into pudding, and I don't want to draw the attention of Silthar just yet. I have many things to do. So long, for now, we'll see each other soon. I'm sure of it."

With a snap of her fingers, she and Vedus were gone, along with the shadows and the pain that wracked Esta's mind.

The Lord-Sire stood, and with a grunt, she pressed a hand to her head and said, "Did that go well?"

Honesty bled from her tone as Sana replied, "I don't know."

Esta kneeled next to the dead form of Telrokas and said, "We did it. We're finally free."

The Lord-Sire looked up and saw Sana beam with joy as she replied, "Indeed we are. But we cannot stand on ceremony. We cannot rest until the Nocturnal is brought to his knees before Silthar and faces judgement."

Sana stepped to the throne that crested the other four and eased into it. Though it was bigger than her, Sana easily filled the space with grace and poise. Once, Esta thought her to be a mistaken ruler amongst their fellow vampires. Now she knew that Sana was the only successor that could follow her father should he be dead or otherwise.

Sana looked to the windows on the other side of the room and said, "Celebrate with the bloodlines. Drink in the revelry of our victory for now. I will join you all soon."

Esta bowed and left Sana to ruminate. It has been far too long since any of them could take a moment to drink in their success. Esta would take advantage of this to its fullest. Pride broke within her; Ezran would be proud.

***

Standing amidst familiar shadows, Vastra looked down upon the fallen city of Zelekriv. The Sanguinaire revelled openly in the streets, and even she could hear their shouts and cries of victory.

The wind whipped against her black hood, no ire or sadness overtook her thoughts. Only disappointment in the faith she put in Prince Vedus. She thought he could be more robust. She felt that she could halt her mother's plan, albeit temporarily.

They did not know; how could they? Mortals never cared for the practicing of the Gods, let alone anything beyond what their wounded forethought could see past. The Gods' plans evaded them, though, to their credit, some of the Gods sheltered their plans even from their most faithful.

The air warped behind her; she did not even flinch as she felt his presence behind her. She would have welcomed it any time before but not now.

He said, "Thalyssra. What news do you have?"

She shook her head, "I couldn't stop him. I couldn't stop her. Her influence was too great. And I've told you before not to call me by that name."

She felt him step closer to her, resting a hand on her shoulder, and said in his all too familiar warm tone, "It is not out of weakness that you have failed. Some things are meant to pass. Even ones we cannot bear to let come to fruition."

Vastra could see the look on his bearded face, a look of wisdom passing on. She knew the look well, and still, she could not help but feel powerless to stop her mother.

She said to him, not moving her gaze from Zelekriv, "I will stop her if it's the last thing I do."

He sat beside her, a groan escaping his lips as the smoke from his pipe filled her lungs. The familiar scent brought calm to her weary thoughts as he said, "And you will, daughter of Daylan. You will. Follow these noblest of people, and you might yet stop your mother."

Vastra finally looked over at him. Ragged cloth with a mantle of raven feathers clung to his powerful but elderly frame. His starry eyes looked down at the burning city as she said, "Noble? They feed off of blood and magical energy. What's noble about that?"

He breathed out another puff of smoke and replied stoically, "They have faced nothing but slavery for the last few centuries. Just because their ways are alien to you or do not align with your morals and understanding does not give you the right to cast judgements. They fought this conflict not to feed their hunger but to fight for their freedom.

"Unburdened by the shackles of their masters to have control of their own destinies. Think not with your preconceived notions, and you might find similarities between yourself and them. Your destiny lies with them and their crusade to retake what rightfully belongs to them."

His heady response caused a headache to form for Vastra. She instead watched Zelekriv hoping that the quiet winds of the mountains could soothe her troubled mind.

In the quiet, he spoke once more and said, "Listen to them. They are the Children of Silthar. What endearing music they make."

www.ingramcontent.com/pod-product-compliance
Lightning Source LLC
Chambersburg PA
CBHW070433170726

48291CB00002B/482